SANDRA BUNINO & LILA SHAW

EVERNIGHT PUBLISHING ®

www.evernightpublishing.com

Copyright© 2018

Sandra Bunino and Lila Shaw

Editor: Karyn White

Cover Artist: Jay Aheer

ISBN: 978-1-77339-817-4

SANDRA BUNINO & LILA SHAW

DEDICATION

Lila Shaw:
My gratitude to Heathcliff, Catherine, Emily Bronte, and Kate Bush. And to my motorcycle-riding Silverback, "don't try this at home."

Sandra Bunino:
To CT & RW, lifelong friends and partners in inappropriate texts.

SANDRA BUNINO & LILA SHAW

NON-RETURNABLE

Club Wars, 1

Sandra Bunino and Lila Shaw

Copyright © 2018

Chapter One

Diesel shifted his legs, giving the hot set of lips access to his balls. He grabbed a chunk of neon blue hair as willing eyes tipped upward, seeking approval. "That's right, baby. Keep going." He cupped her mascara-tracked cheek, guiding the wet and wild ride over his cock. Her inexperience became painfully clear by the light graze of bottom teeth on his flesh, but he had to give her extra points for enthusiasm and creativity as she ran her nails under his balls with one hand and palmed his sack in the other. He tightened his grip as her cheeks hollowed in preparation. Maybe she wasn't as green as he thought. He pumped his hips upward as he exploded into her throat. More points for Blue. She palmed his pulsing shaft and licked away the last of his seed. Diesel nodded toward door at the other end of his office. "Get yourself cleaned up in the bathroom and go out and tell Flint to give you a good spot in tonight's line-up."

She wiped her mouth with the back of her hand. "Really? I made it? I'm a Heather?" Her squeaky voice bounced around the edges of his brain resurrecting the headache he'd had all day.

"Yeah. The boys will love you."

A smile crossed her lips showcasing a set of crooked teeth explaining his sore cock as he zipped up. Poor girl. She could've used the services of an orthodontist. He could tell she came from the proverbial "wrong side of the tracks", and in Detroit, there was an actual wrong side and a right side. Those on the wrong side had little money for necessities, let alone straightening their kids' teeth. Even though Diesel had lived in the gritty city his whole life, he'd never belonged to any side. He floated invisibly over the tracks, yanked from one foster home to another, never staying too long in any of them to call them home.

The muffled sounds of a toilet flush and running water signaled him Blue was almost ready for her Detroit Auto Friday night party debut. Fridays were dedicated to the fully patched members of the Heathen Brotherhood MC, and one of the many perks of membership was the parties complete with strippers. They gave the guys a night without their old ladies, and, as President of the club, Diesel got his cock sucked. The Heathens were big on tradition, and tradition had it that in order to dance on Friday night, new girls, or Heathers, had to successfully blow the president. Who was Diesel to argue with tradition?

The rusty hinges squeaked as the bathroom door opened, and her bony form slipped into the room. "T-thank you, Mr. Diesel," she said as her eyes darted away as soon as he met her gaze.

"Call me Diesel. No Mister. Okay, Blue?"

Her eyes blanked. "Blue? Oh! 'Cuz my hair." She tugged a straggly lock at her shoulder and giggled.

He chuckled. She'd be someone's old lady in no

time. "Yeah, because of your hair. Go talk to Flint and tell him to have one of the boys grill you a cheeseburger. You can use some meat on those bones."

Diesel never understood why girls wanted to be so fucking skinny. He preferred his women with curves. He needed something to hold onto that felt like he wouldn't break it in two. Like his life, Diesel liked his sex rough and dirty, and he needed someone who'd take it all and crave for more.

Her hand moved to her concave belly between her tiny shirt and low-slung jeans. "I am a little hungry."

He nodded, and a sharp pain hit his own stomach. The girl probably hadn't had a decent meal in a long time, and a few minutes ago his only concern was shooting cum down her throat. "How old are you?" Diesel knew she was at least eighteen. The Heathens' officers knew not to allow underage girls inside. The club's monthly stipend to the Detroit PD was high enough, and they kept their bargain: no underage sex and no prostitution.

"I'll be nineteen next month." It was usually about the age the local girls came sniffing around the club. After graduating high school, their options were limited to working a shitty minimum wage job or prostitution. Becoming a Heather upped the chance of becoming a Heathen old lady, which was like winning the lottery for some.

A deep bass beat sounded through the wall. "The party's getting started. Go out there and find Flint."

She smiled again and dashed to the door.

The music pounded his brain as she raced out, and he was happy to be alone in his office. He adjusted his aching cock and strode to the refrigerator, pulling a can of beer from one of the cases. He popped it open and stood in front of the window overlooking the fenced backlot, which housed their recent acquisitions and his prized 1969 Dodge Charger. The lot used to be packed, but over the past few months the number of cars had dwindled. Diesel drained his beer, closed his fist around the empty can, and chucked the gnarled ball into the corner with the other two he'd guzzled earlier in the hopes of dulling the edge off his shitty day. Fuck, it'd been a shitty week rounding out a shitty month.

The noises of the party invaded his ears as the door opened and closed. Diesel didn't have to turn away from the window to know who had just entered his office. Flint was like clockwork, and it was time for Diesel's weekly status report. The man who acted as the Heathens' club secretary and treasurer slumped into the worn leather couch and lowered the pair of glasses from his head to the bridge of his nose as he flipped through the creased paper.

"No question about it. Sales are in the crapper again this month." He tossed the packet of paper on the table. "We're not bringing the cars in like we used to. No cars to chop, no parts to sell."

Detroit Auto not only served as the Heathens' clubhouse, but it was also the main source of income for the club and some of its members. About a dozen fully patched members were on the payroll as mechanics, bodyworkers, and guys in charge of churning the inventory for profit. Once the biggest aftermarket parts dealer in the state, business had plummeted so much over the past six months, Diesel had to yet again kick in his own money to make payroll and the monthly contribution to the Detroit PD's "shut the fuck up and look the other way" fund.

"Did you get the new girl a burger?"

"For fuck's sake, Diesel, did you hear what I said?"

Diesel turned and met Flint's stare. He was the only guy Diesel took shit from. He had ten years and thousands of Heathen ride miles over Diesel. He would've won the presidency during their last election, but Flint didn't want the head position. He was a self-described operations guy. Diesel strode to the table and grabbed the report. There was nothing in it he didn't already know. The Gargoyles were steadily moving in on their turf.

"Maybe I should've taken over as Prez when I had the chance," Flint muttered.

"You want it? At this point, I'd gladly hand the job over to you, start that new chapter in Milwaukee we've been talking about for over a year. Just say the word." He paused long enough for Flint to backpedal with a snort and a shake of his head. "No? It's not an easy fix, and you know it." The Gargoyles were a young club compared to the decades of Heathen membership. The two clubs started off amicably, and Diesel threw some goodwill their way by giving them a small piece of the car business but like all young brats, they'd overstepped their welcome.

"Just don't go soft on us. There's no room in The Brotherhood for a soft prez."

"Fuck yourself, Flint. I'm not soft. I'm smart, and I don't want any of our guys in jail … or dead. Spider is a crazy motherfucker, but we gotta keep the blood off our hands."

Flint poked his thumb over his shoulder. "You know the club is losing respect. They can't wait much longer. They're sayin' you keep drawing the line, but the Gargoyles keep crossing it, taking our turf and our business. Maybe it's time we clued them in."

Diesel's brow furrowed. "We're in too deep and too close to the payoff to change tracks now. It's too risky. We can't afford any kind of a leak that'll get back to Spider or the Gargoyles."

Flint shook his head and sighed, eyes slowly closing in that disappointed way he had. The Heathens had forged a quid pro quo but very off the record partnership with the Detroit PD, and keeping it off the radar was why it had been so successful. The Heathens had doubled their net take since that first handshake and business was going great, until Spider began biting the hand that fed him. Once upon a time Diesel had naively thought the Gargoyles and Heathens might merge, but that was before Spider took over as president. Diesel's plans got royally fucked up when that happened.

"Okay, but if the guys pissin' and moanin' ain't enough to change your mind, how about this?" Flint leaned back and fished his smartphone from his pocket. Squinting at the device he slowly scrolled through his feed and tapped his meaty thumb on the screen. "Here." He tossed his phone to Diesel.

His eyes tipped to the display, which was cued on an article from the Free Press.

Local Teen Dead from Overdose

"This shit happens all the time in this fucking city. What's this have to do with anything?" Diesel asked.

"Read it, asshole."

Diesel quickly scanned the article. A sixteen year old with no history of drug abuse was found dead in her home. When questioned, her friends reported she was seeing a biker who was pressuring her to sell heroin to her classmates. The two were spotted arguing on school property hours before she was found dead. The man had not yet been identified, but police were investigating the two outlaw motorcycle clubs in the city. Two clubs.

Diesel chucked the phone to Flint. "This wasn't one of our guys. Cops should already know that."

"Course it wasn't one of ours. Our guys know the rules. But the girl's family and the public are already all over this, putting pressure on the Mayor to crack down on *all* the MCs, whether guilty or not."

Diesel rubbed his palm over his face. "The Gargoyles just broke two of the golden rules. No underage girls and no drugs. One more reason they gotta go."

"When's somebody gonna get off their ass and do something about it?"

Diesel never thought he'd be so tired at thirty-one. He didn't need Flint to tell him his brothers were growing tired of waiting on him to act, tired of being told to be patient, that he was working on a plan. He couldn't blame them, but if he could convince them to sit tight another week, two tops, the Gargoyles would be history and the Heathens would emerge better than before.

"We have to be smart about this, keep our noses clean. It's not as simple as a bar fight and smashing faces. Anyone surviving that sting gets a whiff it was the Heathens that helped the cops and we go to war. That's not going to solve anything."

"In my day that's exactly how we solved this sort of thing. Ranger just did a drive-by. The Gargoyles' shop is mostly empty. One bike and a couple of cars. He said Spider's hot cup of sweet mocha just walked in. Python thinks we should pay her a visit."

Diesel glared at Flint. "Python doesn't call the shots." His mentor was right though. He had to give them an outlet for their frustrations. Maybe he could also test their loyalty and ability to keep their mouths shut with a low stakes op directed at the Gargoyles. But he'd have to do it without hurting the one person he'd promised himself to protect. "End the party and get the girls and the prospects out. I'm calling a members-only meeting.

Fully patched guys only. Everyone else leaves."

"What for?" Flint asked, his brows knitted.

"I'm going to give them a distraction," Diesel said.

Flint locked gazes with Diesel and after a few heady seconds of visible doubt, finally nodded and left the room. His voice boomed, and the music stopped, followed by a scuffle of activity. Diesel grabbed his vest and helmet and joined everyone in the meeting room as the members took seats or stood in groups of two or three. All eyes shifted to him as he took his place at the front of the room.

"Listen up. You know we've given the Gargoyles some slack with turf boundaries since they're the new brats on the block." A low rumble traveled through the circle. It wasn't a secret many of the members weren't in favor of his decision, never wanted anything to do with a possible club merger, a fact Flint reminded him of almost daily. "But they've fucked up too many times. You all heard about the local high school girl who OD'd. They're looking for an unidentified biker as the source of the heroin, which means our club will be crawling with the DPD any minute."

"Whata we doin' about it?" Python, Heathens' Sergeant-at-Arms, growled.

"First we need to clean house. I want it to look like we're fucking knitting baby blankets in here. I need our best choppers to break down the hot cars in the back. We can't have any evidence of illegal activity until this thing blows over. Only patches in the club until further notice and no girls in here unless they belong to Heathen members."

Python lumbered around the group and assigned jobs to a dozen men who scattered to their tasks. He strode to Diesel's side. "You want me to pull the A-team?" Python's voice rumbled close. Diesel nodded once. The officers of the club had a code red plan prepared, including which members they'd take into their inner circle for certain situations. As much as Diesel wished he could share information about the undercover operation with his A-team, he couldn't risk it, for all the reasons he'd shared with Flint.

In the meantime, he would have to keep them focused on what he'd paint as a credible threat from the cops and public opinion. If the Gargoyles were also dealing drugs, their takedown would be even more satisfying and, he hoped, more imminent.

"Pitfall, Breakneck, Opal, Speed, and Ranger, stay. The rest of you, help the choppers. We need this place looking respectable in an hour."

Most of the group dispersed, leaving the men Diesel trusted more than anything in life. Those guys were his family, they all were, but especially the small group surrounding him.

"What's the plan, boss?" Python asked with eager eyes. The biker lived for these moments. Like, Diesel, Python was single. And also like Diesel, his life was The Brotherhood.

"We put a lookout outside their clubhouse and we wait until Spider's alone."

Python shook his head. "Wait a fucking minute. Your plan is to clean up our place and put eyes on Spider. That's it?"

"For now."

"They're gonna keep taking what's ours until we have nothing left. They need to be stopped. Tonight."

Grunts of agreement traveled around the circle of men.

"Nothing's happening tonight. It's too dangerous."

"You're not one to drag your feet, Diesel. What

the hell?"

"We know Spider doesn't play by the rules. We're gonna strike soon, but I'm not about to risk our men or our club. There's too much at stake." Diesel's gaze traveled around the group, and a sliver of unease crept up his spine. They weren't buying what he was shoveling. He didn't care. "We'll meet again tomorrow," Diesel said and headed toward the door. He needed air.

"This is bullshit," Python hissed under his breath.

Diesel turned to face his Sergeant-at-Arms. "My club. My law," Diesel said evenly.

Chapter Two

Spider was at it again, the fucking asshole. And in their bed, too! Using the tips of two fingers, Cathy picked up the pair of women's panties that had tumbled from the sheets after she stripped the bed. They definitely weren't hers. For starters, she never wore sheer black nylon with a gap where the crotch should be. They were also way too small for her more substantial assets. What to do with the evidence though?

From past experience, her tearful confrontations ended one of two ways: Spider would apologize, usually after swearing it didn't mean anything, and then purchase her more jewelry that she would only wear once before chucking his guilt gift into her already overflowing jewelry box. The second would be him hurling recriminations at her, why her failures as a woman had left him no choice. She was too fat, too selfish, too moody, too smitten with some imaginary lover he accused her of having stashed away somewhere. Like, how would that ever happen? She rarely got to leave the house or the club.

Both scenarios sucked.

But what sucked even more was she wasn't sure she even cared. If he was off fucking some other Bunny, he wasn't nagging at her to give him head, let him fuck her up the ass or his most recent idea—a three-way as an initiation for the latest Bunny. Heaven forbid he suggest a three-way with a male initiate. That might stir her blood a little more than eating some other woman's pussy.

Cathy tossed the panties in the trash and covered them up with used tissues and other garbage already in the can. Some things were better left to die a quiet death. These sorts of annoyances came with the territory, unfortunately, and Spider and all the boys got themselves tested regularly and used protection. She wouldn't stake her life on it, but what else could she do? She had nowhere else to go, no job, no family. Spider and the rest of the Gargoyles were her family. Nobody ever said family was perfect and hers certainly was no exception, but she loved them, she guessed. She didn't know for sure. There was only one person she could say for certain she'd ever loved, but he was a distant memory from a lifetime ago. Spider and his whole family had been with her through some difficult times. She owed them loyalty.

A flash of orange plastic flipped to the top of the garbage after she'd buried the panties. She grasped it only to discover it was a recapped syringe. A syringe? In her garbage can?

What. The. Fuck? Was Spider doing drugs now? Surely, he wouldn't be that stupid. Maybe he was diabetic and hadn't told her? Like that would happen. He was a hypochondriac who demanded she be his nursemaid at the slightest sniffle or headache. "Make me some chicken soup. Rub my legs. Massage my temples. Bring me the ledgers. Tell so and so to do this and that." He ran her ragged. No, if Spider was on insulin, he damn sure would have told her and he'd have made a big fucking Broadway show out of it.

Did it belong to the Bunny Spider had fucked in their bed? Had Spider given her the drugs, or worse, shot up, too? Cathy's blood raged through her veins, her heart pounding in her ears. No condom in the world would protect Spider from Hep C or HIV delivered via needle. Surely, he wouldn't be that stupid.

If only she knew what had been in the syringe. Was there anyway she could tell? Unlike the cops on television, she had no idea what heroin tasted like, and she for damn sure would never experiment, certainly not with a used needle. But maybe one of the other old ladies of the club could help. Lucy came to mind first. She was Dagger's old lady. Dagger was the Sergeant-at-Arms and one of the longest running members of the Gargoyles. He'd even recruited Spider, and her since they were a package deal, into the club. Best thing about Lucy, however, was she kept her mouth shut and could be trusted not to go ratting her out to Dagger, who would ultimately tell Spider. She'd know if the boys had connections to the drug market—something Spider swore to her he'd never dabble in.

Cathy found an unused tampon and discarded the insert, retaining the applicator. She slipped the syringe's orange tip inside the plastic applicator and then wrapped it up in several tissues before stashing it inside her purse. A quick glance at her watch confirmed Lucy would be at the club by now. On Monday nights the old ladies usually drove themselves to the club because the guys had business they conducted in the "field". The guys typically streamed in on their hogs around seven. She'd have a good thirty minutes if she left immediately.

She paused at the door to the downtown condo she shared with Spider and took in a deep breath. As she exhaled, she mentally shifted gears to assume her role in the club as Thorn, Spider's old lady. All her years in foster care had given her a chameleon-like ability to be who she needed to be to fit in, be accepted, survive.

****

Thorn parked on the side of the Gargoyles' body shop that also served as their clubhouse. A quick inventory of the vehicles—auto and motorcycle—told her Lucy was inside. PeeWee's Harley was the only one of the guys' bikes parked in the area. Who knew why he'd be at the club? Something about PeeWee made her uneasy, almost as if he were a cop or a spy or something.

To Thorn, it seemed he was always skulking around, lurking in every conversation, even the old ladies'! They called him PeeWee because he was only five foot six and had the typical short man's syndrome to match. He always had a barb to toss at Thorn in particular, who being two inches taller, towered over him when in heels. She suspected other parts of PeeWee were tiny, too, but that was a mystery she preferred to leave unsolved.

PeeWee was the first to greet her at the door. "Hey, Thorn. How's it going?" he asked looking her up and down in a way that made her skin crawl.

"Fine. You seen Lucy?" She avoided eye contact and scanned the garage and the hallway to the back club room. She also kept moving, but PeeWee kept pace with her, obviously in the mood to talk.

"She's in the back. That a new blouse you're wearing? It's very … colorful."

"Nope, not new at all." She didn't want to engage with PeeWee and needed to get rid of him so she could talk to Lucy without him eavesdropping. Stopping, she said, "Hey, PeeWee, do me a favor and bring in the beer I brought." She dangled her keys in his face.

PeeWee's phony smile morphed into a genuine one. He took the keys. "Now that's an errand I'll run for anyone, even an old lady."

Thorn tossed him a thank you smile, turned and entered the club room. "Hey, Lucy," she said.

"Thorn! Looking good, mama!"

Three other old ladies—Harriet, Ethel, and Ricki—sat together on the sofa watching some house flipping show on HGTV, enthralled by the flippers' squabbles over the perfect kitchen countertops. Lucy sat at the kitchen table, eating a salad. Thorn slipped into the chair next to her.

In a lowered voice, Thorn asked, "Have you

heard anything about the boys dealing or using drugs?"

Lucy's eyes widened. "What kind of drugs? Meth? Dope? Heroin? Pills?"

"I think heroin." Thorn double-checked the hallway for PeeWee and cast a glance at the other old ladies. "I found a syringe in the garbage can."

"Which garbage can? Here at the club?" From the shocked expression on Lucy's face, Thorn had little doubt that Lucy knew nothing, and if Lucy didn't know, chances were the syringe she found had nothing to do with the club. A wave of relief washed over her.

"Not here. In my condo." Thorn again cast her gaze about the area to check for listeners. "Keep this on the DL, though, would you? Don't mention it to Dagger or anyone else."

Lucy's brow furrowed and the corners of her lips turned downward. "What do you think it means? What are you going to do?"

"I don't know. I need to find out more."

"Are you going to confront Spider?" she asked in a whisper.

"God, no," Thorn replied in an equally soft whisper. "I'll just keep my eyes and ears open. You do the same, okay?"

"Sure, sure, but what about—"

She never finished her sentence because the room was plunged into darkness followed by a loud crash in the garage.

Chapter Three

The sleepless night spent tossing and turning only fueled Diesel's foul mood as he dragged his ass back to the clubhouse early the next morning. His lids may as well have been lined with sandpaper as he rubbed the grit from his eyes and cursed the bikes already in the fence-bordered lot. He figured he'd have time to think before the others arrived. His gaze drifted to Python's bike, a rare sighting before noon. His gut clenched as he drew air into his lungs. He couldn't shake the unease crawling up his spine.

Diesel paused at the side door before jamming his key into the lock. The door sounded a metal on metal squeal as he stepped into the dark hallway leading to the club's offices and meeting room. None of the normal daily noises were present. No drone of stupid television game shows the guys had become hooked on, no revving motors or purring saws. Nothing. His footsteps sounded on the unswept concrete floor. As he was about to turn the knob, the door to his office flew open. Diesel's gaze jumped from Python's steely eyes to Flint whose forehead creased into a roadmap of lines.

"Diesel," Flint said, clearly rattled as he stepped from the office followed by Python.

"Why are you two in so early?"

Python squared his shoulders. "Takin' care of some business. Come on, we'll fill you in," he said, yanking the door closed.

Flint rubbed his palm over his face. "Gotta make some breakfast."

Diesel followed the men into the kitchen. He leaned against the counter as Flint pulled the refrigerator door open and dropped a carton of eggs and a slab of bacon on the counter. He rummaged through the cabinet for a pan while Python took his time measuring coffee grounds for the machine. "Why have you two suddenly turned into hairy versions of Martha Stewart? Is someone going to tell me what the fuck is going on?"

Python poked the button of the coffee maker and slumped into a worn barstool across from Diesel. "You know the group wasn't in agreement with your decision to do nothing about the turf war with the Gargoyles."

"My decision was to get our shit together within our club before we took any steps against them. With that girl's death, the cops could come in and shut us down on the smallest infraction. We don't have that kinda payoff money." Diesel turned to Flint. "You of all people know that."

Flint mumbled something about a distraction under his breath and cracked eggs into a pan.

Python nodded. "You said that. In fact, you *keep* saying that. In the meantime, Spider continues taking our business. How are we supposed to make coin if those douchebags keep picking off what's rightfully ours? I don't get it, and the rest of the guys don't either. I heard some of the younger members were thinking of changing sides."

Diesel huffed a sarcastic chuckle. "Let 'em go. Spider's running that club into the ground. If any of our guys think they'll have it better over there, I'll hold the fucking door open for them."

"You don't get it. These guys only understand an eye for an eye. That's how they were raised. That's what they do. All this waiting around until the fucking moon aligns with Jupiter before Diesel decides he's ready to slap Spider's wrist is bullshit. Something had to be done."

Diesel took a deep breath as his stare shifted from Flint to Python. "*Had* to be done? So you went behind my back."

Python shrugged. "The way I saw it, we had no other choice."

Diesel narrowed his eyes and took a step forward. He grabbed the edge of the counter to stop himself from knocking the smug grin from Python's lips. "What did you do?" he asked evenly.

"You always say we gotta get the enemy where it hurts," Python said and turned his gaze to Flint, who plated an army's supply of scrambled eggs and bacon onto a platter.

"I'm going to ask one more time. What the fuck did you do?" He pointed to the platter. "And who's all that food for?" Diesel's mind raced in a million directions, all of them to places he wasn't ready to go.

Flint lifted the platter and jerked his head toward the hallway. "Grab the OJ," he directed Diesel.

Diesel snagged the carton of orange juice from the counter with one hand and pulled a bottle of Stoli from the shelf with the other. He had the feeling he'd need it. He followed the two men back to his office. A muffled thud sounded from inside as Python opened the door.

"Who's in there?" Diesel asked. An icy blast zipped up his spine.

"We have a couple of guests staying at the Heathen B&B," Python said.

A whimper sounded from the corner, and Diesel froze. "What the fuck have you done?" It was a question he didn't need an answer to as his eyes adjusted to the dim lighting of the room. Two forms hooded in dark sheets were seated on his desk chairs facing the wall. Their muffled whimpers increased as he stepped forward.

"Breakfast is served, ladies. I don't want you to think we don't have manners here," Flint said and set the tray of food on Diesel's desk.

"Are you out of your fucking minds? Who are they?"

Python strode to the captives' chairs and turned each around so they faced Diesel. "May I introduce you to Lucy, also known as Dagger's old lady." He pulled the hood from one of the forms. A shock of red hair billowed around the woman's face, the duct tape gag she wore stifling her words but not her growls. Eyes cold as Lake Michigan hooked onto Diesel's. "And the juicy flower of Spider's life, Thorn."

A guttural mix of rage and surprise exploded as the hood was pulled from the other. Diesel's gaze locked on eyes he knew too well. Eyes that had been capable of reading his thoughts before he even knew them. Those eyes grabbed hold of his, and in a second, he knew they were still able to do exactly that. He was screwed.

Diesel tore his gaze from Thorn's. He needed a plan. Fast. He stuck his index finger in Flint's direction. "Stay here until I get back. We're going to have another long chat about patience." Then he threw a nod at Python. "You. Come with me."

Diesel strode to the dark garage. The heels of his boots echoed angrily on the concrete floor. He flipped the light switch as the steel door slammed shut behind him. He turned to Python who squinted under the unyielding bright lights. "You on something?" It wasn't the first time he wondered if Python had started using again.

Python shook his head. "I'm clean, man."

"Was I not clear last night when I said we were gonna get together this morning before taking any kind of action?"

"The opportunity came up. I took it. I was protecting our club, something you seem to give zero fucks about."

Diesel slammed his fist on a tool bench, scattering a collection of wrenches to the ground. "Protecting? You've put this club in danger by breaking the treaty."

"It was the only way to make the Gargoyles stand up and take notice. They broke it first, and they've been shitting on us for months. There's no respect there. They're doing whatever the fuck they want. Fuck the treaty!"

"No. *You're* doing whatever the fuck you want. This club has rules for a reason. We make decisions together."

Python took a step toward Diesel. "Together," he repeated with a sarcastic chuckle. "It was *your* decision for us to sit here with our thumbs up our asses because of some pansy-ass treaty while the Gargoyles staked a claim right under our noses. You didn't ask any of us what we wanted. You let them steal our turf, our livelihood, our respect. You think no one's talking about it? They're waiting for you to do something. I did what you're too much of a pussy to do."

Rage coursed through Diesel's veins. He threw his tightened fist square into Python's jaw. The biker fell to the ground. "Jeezus," he muttered holding his split lip.

"Never disobey me," Diesel said evenly and strode to the door.

"Diesel," Python said stumbling to his feet. "You're the president. Start fucking acting like it." He spat blood that landed a foot away from Diesel's boot.

"As Sergeant-at-Arms, you're supposed to be a leader in this club. Be part of the team or get the fuck out. Your choice," Diesel said yanking the door and letting it clang shut behind him. Python had always had his back in the past, and it was the only reason he didn't throw him out of the club. He let him off easy with the blow to his jaw, but it was enough collateral damage to show the other members Diesel wouldn't stand for dissent in the ranks. He raked his hand over his face and headed to deal with the fire raging in his office.

****

Thorn blinked to ward off the daggers of light flooding her eyes. The drugs the intruders had used to knock her out had finally surrendered their hold on her consciousness, but her muscles still felt the draining weakness. Men. Strangers. They had invaded the club in a fury of shouts and brandished pistols. With only PeeWee on duty—who, she recalled with disgust, had passively taken a seat and cooperated—they had been outnumbered and easily captured. The knock out drugs they used had further ensured an easy operation.

The men had snatched at least one other person, but his or her identity was a mystery until the sheet covering her had been pulled off. She turned her head and spotted a gagged and furious Lucy sitting next to her. *What the ever-loving fuck?*

Thorn drew in a shuddering breath through her nose, and with eyes closed forced down the fear that clawed for an escape. When she finally opened her eyes again, through her clearing vision her gaze locked with his.

Dear God, those eyes.

She'd never forgotten them. How could she? They belonged to the man she had both loved and loathed equally. But he was dead to her now just as she was dead to him. He'd hammered in the last nail in both their coffins years ago. No crying. Not anymore. Not ever again and certainly not when crying would stuff up her nose and possibly choke off her sole airway given the very tight strip of duct tape sealing her mouth.

He stared back at her, and other than the nearly

indiscernible tell she remembered, he said nothing, gave no hint of recognition. But he did know who she was. Of that she was sure. She could only hope he gave no voice to his recognition. She would hold her peace, wouldn't surrender the satisfaction of feigned indifference. He was dead to her.

One of the other men walked over and ripped off the tape from Lucy's face.

"What's going on?" Lucy shrieked. "You sons of bitches. You're all going to die when Dagger and Spider find out."

The man ripped off hers, too, and holy Baby Jesus did it hurt. Thorn took a deep breath in through her mouth while Lucy continued to rage at their captors. Deep breath in—Spider would rescue them—deep breath out—these men would pay dearly—quick breath in—and she didn't, wouldn't care about any of them—long, slow breath out. *Be calm. Don't give them the satisfaction of your anger or fear.*

"Where are we? What do you fuckers want?" Thorn directed her words and gaze to the man she had once known as Trey. Least of all him, she would not give him her fear. Nor her recognition. Nor any emotion. He didn't even deserve to be spat upon.

Lucy let out another screech and struggled against her restraints. Like Thorn, she'd also been duct-taped with arms at her sides, layers and layers of tape around her chest and the back of the chair. They'd done the same with their legs, binding them at the ankles to the base of the wheeled chair. Her captors didn't appear to be in any hurry to remove those.

"Lucy, hush. Remember the pact." Thorn was referring to their contingency plan. All the members had standing rules about what to say and do if arrested by the police or taken hostage by a rival gang. Though the rules were slightly different for the women, the unified message was to offer no information about the club or its members, demand the club's lawyer if arrested, cite the turf law and consequences to rival gang members, never acquiesce. The overarching theme was defiance even in the face of death. No fear. No crying. No anger. Thorn added to that, no recriminations and no second chances.

Trey's jaw tightened. "Separate them," he barked to the other man. "I don't want them colluding. Put that one," he pointed to Lucy, "in the storage room. Leave this one here with me. Alone. She and I are going to have a little chat." He raked his gaze over her body with a deliberate and heaping dose of lust. The sweaty man who smelled like beer and onions dutifully grabbed Lucy's chair and began to roll her out as she screamed and cursed the entire way, leaving Thorn with the cruelest creature on God's green earth. She wished he smelled like beer and onions, too. The stench would make it easier to turn away from him. Her mind repeated all the reasons to hate him, but her traitorous body didn't give a shit about the past or her broken heart or the club's standing rules.

Chapter Four

Don't say anything! Don't believe anything he says. You already know what a lying bastard he is. Remember the plan. No fear. No regrets.

Trey walked closer. Thorn fixed her attention on the edge of the desk. *Keep calm. Say nothing. You don't have to listen to him, not ever again. Ignore. Ignore. Ignore.*

"Cathy?"

Thorn's head jerked up, like a reflex she was powerless to control. She met his gaze. *Dammit! Strike one.* But gone was the leering would-be rapist of thirty seconds ago. In his place was a man wearing a tortured expression.

Oh, fuck me. No. No. Don't. Just ... don't. You will not feel even one fucking iota of empathy for him. Her inner voice continued to chide her, but it was too late. She remembered how his emotions could play across his face, soften the hard edges he wore like armor. She was seeing them now, those hints of the boy of her childhood. Trey had always been an open book to her—back then, before he shuttered up and then left her without a word.

The man in front of her might look like the Trey of her childhood, but he wasn't. He was Diesel of the Heathens. She'd known about his new identity for some time, but had pushed any awareness of him into the farthest corners of her mind. Trey's alter ego, Diesel, was like a zombie to her, both familiar and deadly.

"You okay? Did they hurt you?" Trey's voice was low and even, but his fists clenched at his sides. "I'll fucking waste any of them that so much as scratched you."

"Is there such a thing as a white glove

abduction?"

His features locked back into the hardened expression of a warrior. Thorn swallowed a lump of regret at seeing the ghost of Trey so quickly vanquished. The glimpse of him had been only that—a glimpse—but Thorn reminded herself of the club's pact. She also reminded herself that this man was her enemy and would never be anything else.

Diesel perched a hip on the corner of the desk, inches away from her. "For what it's worth, this wasn't my idea. I had no idea you or Lucy had been taken until I walked in this room."

"Your apology isn't worth shit unless you release us before the Gargoyles can strike back."

He drew in a deep breath. His gaze skittered about the room. Despite her tough talk, Thorn wondered how the President of the Heathens could not have known about the kidnappings, if he was telling her the truth or if he was only trying to use their past to get her to talk. Isolate her. Dredge up old memories to retrigger her addiction. Schmooze her into giving up information about Spider and the Gargoyles.

"I didn't apologize," he said with a smirk. He picked up the bottle of Stoli on his desk and unscrewed the cap. He shook his head and whipped the bottle across the room, smashing it against the wall where it exploded into a million pieces. "You being here fucks up my end game as much as it does yours. I have nothing to gain and everything to lose from this cock and bullshit those morons dumped on me."

Thorn refused to show him how much his actions rattled her. "We're cock and bullshit? Lovely." Thorn torn her gaze from his and searched for an alternate, safer focal point. Unfortunately, with him sitting on the edge of the desk so close, the bulge in his loose-fitting jeans drew her attention. They were well-worn and faded in the usual spots from true wear and not the faux designer streaks and whiskers—the hems, the knees eroded to horizontal white threads that allowed a peek of skin and the area next to his zipper. He very obviously dressed left. She closed her eyes and frantically tried to erase the image before it could burn into her memory, but her imagination had already begun running with it.

Focus, Thorn!

****

The woman he'd only know as Cathy turned her head to pointedly scan the room before locking a pair of dark, narrowed eyes on him and saying, "That greaseball better not touch Lucy."

Diesel couldn't hide his grin, which judging by the daggers she threw his way with her stare, was wrongly perceived.

"I swear I'll kill you. Or have you killed. If anything happens to her—"

Her eyes welled with tears, transporting him more than a decade into the past to the dark basement of his seemingly hundredth, but last, foster home. Only it wasn't just his foster home, it was hers, too. He knew she was the lucky one. She was about to be adopted, but he'd also known she didn't see it that way. Diesel was on the cusp of eighteen and about to age out of the system. Cathy begged him to take her along, but at sixteen she still had a chance of a family. He refused to rob her of the thing she'd always so desperately wanted. He remembered her tearful pleas.

"Please, Trey! You can't leave me here alone. You're all I have. All that I've ever loved. You love me, too. I know you do. You told me so."

He'd never forget or forgive his response.

"Come on, Cath. You didn't believe me, did you?

Never believe a guy who says he loves you before or while he's fucking you. You better smarten up fast, girl. I don't love you. I never have. You were just an easy lay."

"But all those things we talked about. Being together, making a life together. They were all lies?"

Her tear-stained face remained seared in his brain forever. But she was different now. Her eyes hadn't changed, but everything else had. No longer a girl, her luscious curves were those of a woman. Instead of a slumped posture in an attempt to blend into the backdrop and not call attention to herself as she did as a teen, this Cathy sat up straight, challenging him with squared shoulders and the experience of someone much older than her twenty-nine years. It was like a stab to his gut. She was so strong, but she had an icy edge he wondered if his past actions helped put into place when he broke her heart all those years ago. She claimed he left her with nothing, but the truth was he'd left her with the promise of a family.

"Flint's an old-timer. He respects women. Nothing like those young buck assholes your boyfriend recruits into the Gargoyles. Trust me, Lucy's safe under Flint's watch."

"Oh, you want me to trust you? Now that's rich. Fool me once, shame on you. Fool me twice, shame on me." She looked away and bit her lip, seemingly regretting her last remark. He watched her chest rise and fall with a deep breath before she regained his gaze. "What are you going to do with us, Trey?"

The stabbing sensation zipped to his chest at the sound of his real name. It sounded foreign but at the same time so familiar from her lips. He was sure it was a ploy to manipulate him to her advantage.

"What do you think I should do with you?" Turning the question on the other person was a tactic he'd learned a long time ago when he had no answers. Foster Care 101.

"I think you should let us go before Spider and his guys break down your doors and kill you, which, by the way, they may do regardless, in retribution for all this."

"Thanks for the tip. Anything else?"

"Yeah. That food behind you is probably cold, but I'm starving. Care to cut me loose so I can eat?"

He considered her request as his eyes trailed over her body. "You have any weapons on you?"

A brief grin played at her lips. "You scared of me?"

"My day has sucked enough. I'd rather not have a switchblade to my kidneys to top it off."

"No weapons but I doubt you believe me."

"You're right. I'll cut your arms loose but only if you agree to a pat down. Nothing improper. You have my word."

She tilted her head and eyed the platter of food. "If a pat down is the only thing keeping me from that bacon, knock yourself out."

He leaned over and flattened his palms over her shoulders, sliding them slowly down and back up her arm over the sleeve of her shirt. He patted her chest but avoided her bra. She raised her eyebrows. "Don't want to cop a feel? The girls have graduated from training bras," she said flatly.

"Told you I wouldn't do anything improper. But if you pull a knife from your cleavage all bets are off." He dropped to his knees as his palms fell to her thighs. Her jeans were so freaking tight he doubted she had any weapons hidden. Not only would they bulge through the material, she'd have a heck of a time removing them from their hiding spots. He ran his hand up one side and down the other before standing and pulling his own switchblade from his back pocket and sliced through the duct tape imprisoning her arms. She yanked them free and rubbed her wrists. Her feet were still bound to the chair legs, so Diesel pulled her seat closer to the desk.

She reached for a slice of bacon and took a bite. "Can you make sure Lucy gets something to eat? She must be starving, too." It was yet another reminder that tugged him to their past.

"You always did worry about everyone else." The last foster family was in it for the money so they took in as many kids as the state would allow, adding more mouths to feed to their brood of five kids. Cathy often went without breakfast to ensure the younger ones had something to eat before school.

"And you only worried about yourself." She nibbled another slice of bacon and stuck a forkful of scrambled eggs into her mouth before wrinkling her nose. "Mmm, cold, rubbery eggs. My favorite."

Everything about her presence was a cruel reminder of the part of his life he kept buried so deep he didn't even know where to find it. But suddenly it was bubbling to the surface, raw and ragged. He drew himself up from the desk and towered over her, his breath shallow as he tried to rein in the cocktail of emotions swimming inside.

Cathy tossed the fork on the platter. "You gonna hit me, Trey?"

"Do you think I'm a fucking monster?" he yelled as his fist came down hard on the desk, and he flung the tray of food from the surface landing on the floor in a thud of broken glass and congealed eggs. Their gazes locked and held, and he searched her eyes for a flicker of understanding of the torture he endured all those years. But all he received was a cold stare in return. He *was* a monster in her eyes.

A heavy knock pulled his attention to the door. Flint stepped inside, his gaze traveling to the mess on the floor. "Jeezuz, that's the last time I make breakfast," he muttered. "I need to see you in the hall."

Diesel strode toward the door, the crunch of broken glass sounding under his boots. He followed Flint into the hall, leaving the door cracked open a few inches behind him to keep Cathy out of earshot but within eyesight.

"How the fuck did this happen, Flint?" He was practically nose-to-nose with the man. His hands were balled into fists at his sides, still throbbing from his punch to Python's face. He'd deck Flint, too, if it came to that.

"Whoa. Whoa. This was not my idea. You should have heard what Python *wanted* to do! I only went along to keep the others out of it and to make sure he didn't royally fuck stuff up beyond repair. You said you wanted a distraction." Flint waved a hand toward the door. "Well, there you go! There's your plan B."

Diesel thumbed over his shoulder toward the room. "That ain't no plan B. That's a ticking time bomb."

Flint said in a hushed voice, "In other news, our informant at the DPD called. The Gargoyles are trying to frame us for pushing drugs at the high school."

"Why would anyone believe them? Most of Spider's guys have rap sheets longer than the Van Dyke Freeway." Long before Diesel agreed to work with the undercover cop, the Heathen MC had negotiated an arrangement with a private DPD union, men in blue who turned a blind eye for a price. The Heathens limited their illegal business to hot cars, and certain higher-ups on the force got their pockets lined in exchange for looking the other way. Not only did the Gargoyles not have the same relationship, they also couldn't keep their noses clean.

Flint shrugged. "They won't, of course."

Diesel relaxed his hands and slowly nodded as an idea formed. "Right. But it's the type of distraction I was thinking of and will buy us some time." Python's impetuousness had another silver lining. Diesel could leverage it to keep Cathy safe.

"You motherfuckers better let us go now and maybe I'll take pity on you and let you keep your balls!" Lucy shrieked.

Diesel cringed. "Damn, she can hit some high notes."

"Tell me about it. I've been listening to it non-stop for the past twenty minutes. I say we return that one." Flint hoisted his thumb over his shoulder.

Diesel nodded. "You and Python take her back to the Gargoyles. She'll be one less thing to worry about—"

"Do you hear me, fuckers?" Lucy screamed.

"—and listen to," Diesel added.

"What about Spider's old lady? Flint asked.

Diesel craned his neck to get a look at her from the hallway. A judgmental scowl played on her lips and one eyebrow was raised high than the other. "Leave her to me." He knew he'd regret the decision the moment the words left his mouth, but he wasn't about to let her go that easy. Diesel leaned on the doorframe surveying his newest guest. Her eyes narrowed with an unspoken "don't fuck with me" message.

His dick had other ideas.

Chapter Five

"Get your hands off me!"

"Keep bitching and I'll bind and gag you again," Diesel grumbled and tightened his grip on Thorn's forearm as he led her through the garage to the back lot. He opened the passenger door of his prized Dodger Charger and nudged her inside. "Don't piss me off," he warned before closing the door and striding to the driver's side and sliding into the well-worn seat. "Don't try anything stupid. If you do anything that causes damage to this car I won't hesitate to kill you." His eyes flicked to hers, and he could tell she was trying to decide if he was serious.

"Glad to know your priorities are still in the right order," she mumbled and secured her seatbelt.

"Speaking of priorities, you need to put this over your head." He held out a pillowcase.

Thorn crossed her arms and said, "No."

"Put it on or I'll put it on for you after I zip-tie your wrists and ankles. You put the hood on yourself and promise to behave and I'll leave your hands and legs free."

Thorn stared daggers at him. He deflected them right back her way, refusing to blink.

She snatched the pillowcase out of his hand. "Fine. But you're a fucking asshole!"

Once she'd donned the oversized hood that would keep her from discovering the whereabouts of his home, he revved the engine, and an instant shot of adrenaline coursed through his veins. Who needed drugs with a car like his? He didn't take it out much, preferring his bike's gas mileage. Old habits died hard. Growing up with barely a dollar to his name made him frugal, and he never quite got used to having a bank account, let alone a comfortable sum inside it. He pulled out of the lot and after a few turns he could do with his eyes closed, they were soon heading south on the freeway. Diesel could see Thorn's sideways position from the corner of his eye. He imagined Thorn's gaze trying to burn through the sheet and into his head. If anyone could do it, she could. The pillowcase had been necessary for another reason. The least amount of interaction with her was for the best, especially since he had no idea what he was going to do with her or for how long. Fucking Python and his knee-jerk reaction. He dumped a shitstorm in Diesel's lap and expected him to clean it up.

Silence filled the car until she finally shifted forward and ran a hand over the dashboard. "I noticed you got your wish."

"What's that?" he asked.

"This car. You always wanted a vintage Charger."

He rubbed his thumb on the steering wheel. "I wanted a lot of things back then. You did, too. But it looks like you're doing well. You landed the president of the Gargoyles. Life's been good to you."

"If you think being an old lady is everything I want out of life, you don't know me at all."

"We don't know each other, Thorn. We did, but that was a long time ago. People change."

"People don't change. Not really. What changes is what you care to reveal, but inside we're the same."

"I can't believe you remembered I wanted a Charger," Diesel said.

"I remember a lot of things about you," she said softly beneath her hood.

Shit.

"At least more than you remember about me," she added.

"I remember you always had these big thoughts

about life. Always wanted to believe the best in people."

"I was naive. You said it yourself. Look how wrong I was."

Her words sliced his gut wide open, but he quickly recovered, knowing she was baiting him. She was a Gargoyle, and Diesel knew how Outlaw clubs worked. Spider trained her to do whatever was necessary to survive. Heathen old ladies were taught similar rules. Diesel knew them well. Shit, he wrote most of them. Ignoring her comment, he took the next exit.

"Where are you taking me?"

"My place. An address I like to keep private."

"What are you going to do when we get there? What's going to happen to me?"

His head pounded. "Nothing. I'm taking you to my house until I figure this out. It's the only place I know you'll be safe." They wove through residential streets until he pulled into the driveway leading to his house. "We're here. You can take off the hood now."

She did. Her mouth gaped as she leaned forward and stared out the windshield. "This is your place?"

"You look surprised."

"It's just … I didn't think you were, you know, with someone. I heard you were single."

He shot her a grin. "You keeping tabs on me?"

A rosy hue crept up her neck to her cheeks. "No, of course not." She reached a hand up to smooth down the static flyaways and other havoc the hood had caused to her hair. "But once in a while I ask around about you. Making sure you're doing okay, I guess."

"I'm not with someone. I live here alone. Mostly."

"Looks like a nice house."

Like he'd always wanted his car, he always wanted a place he could call his home. When he decided he'd had enough of crashing on the sofa in his office he found a place of his own.

****

Diesel killed the engine inside the cavernous three-car garage. The door groaned down its tracks behind them until metal met cement.

"Wait here," Diesel ordered while wagging his finger at her.

Damn. She hated that imperious finger of his. How many times had he waved it at her when they were kids? She remembered one time when he did, she'd pitched forward fast enough to chomp down on his digit with her teeth. A secret smile stretched her lips. He'd never done it again. Until now. The smile faded into a sigh. Things were different now.

Diesel passed in front of the car to the door that probably led to the interior of his home, tapping at some sort of panel above the doorknob. The door opened, and an excited dog greeted him with yips and a well-choreographed dance on its hind legs. The thing looked like some mixed breed gone horribly wrong—a cropped tail and dwarfed legs like a Corgi, floppy ears like a beagle, and its black and brown coat bore signs of both terrier and poodle. The beast's muzzle was loose and sloppy like a hound's. What the hell kind of dog was it?

But the bigger shock was: Diesel had a dog? Really? She thought MC guys only had pit bulls if they had any pets at all. Spider wasn't a fan of pets. Too much to tie him down, he said, when she'd pleaded for a cat, something low maintenance. He'd calmly shut her down the first time she asked but blown up like Mt. St. Helens the second time she brought it up.

There was no third request. There were no pets. He bought her a bracelet with animal charms instead thinking he'd regained his princely throne in her book. She'd feigned delight, worn the bracelet once, then stashed it away in her jewelry box where it lay semi-forgotten.

Diesel had a dog. *Wow.* It followed him when he turned and walked to her side of the car and opened the door. He made a sweeping gesture with his hand inviting, maybe ordering, her to exit. The dog darted around him, placed a pair of front paws on her knees and dove its head straight into her crotch.

"Dammit! No!" Diesel snapped his fingers.

Thorn laughed but pushed the dog's head away. It dropped back down to all fours and sat, riveted with attention to Diesel. Fortunately, the dog didn't see her as an enemy. "You have a dog?" she said.

"Yes. Dammit's been my girl for the past five years."

Thorn's mouth fell open and she huffed a laugh. "Your dog's name is Dammit?"

Diesel shrugged. "Wasn't intentional. When I first got her and she was a puppy, it seemed like I was always saying, 'Dammit, stop chewing on my shoe!' or 'Dammit, you pissed on the rug again!'. After a while it kinda stuck."

"What was her name supposed to be?"

"I don't even remember," he mumbled as he motioned for her to precede him through the doorway. They entered via a mudroom, or apparently in Diesel's case, a grease room. A laundry basket of dirty rags sat beneath a utility sink, a pair of vintage-looking jackboots to the left of a bench. Above the bench hung several coats of varying styles and degrees of insulation. None of them appeared to belong to a woman. Had he been telling her the truth about not having an old lady?

Thorn continued through and then paused, unsure of whether to go left or right. A warm but firm hand clamped on her shoulder, spun her to the left and nudged her forward, reminding her she wasn't a guest here but a prisoner.

She was heading toward the kitchen. And what a fine one it was, too. Well, fuck him and the horse he rode in on. Money no longer ranked very high on his wish list because clearly he had plenty to burn. Thorn ran a hand over the smooth countertop in the butler's pantry they passed through on their way. Expensive marble, and lots of it. Before her, a gourmet chef's Viking stove with an oversized hood formed the centerpiece of the room. A Sub-Zero refrigerator held court between yards of towering maple cabinets. Hand-carved wood floorings surrounded a massive island flanked by four barstools. Impressive, but she'd have rather died than compliment him on it.

"Sit. Over there." He pointed to a banquette-style dining nook.

Thorn gave him a hard stare that he returned without so much as a blink or twitch. With an audible sigh, she slipped into the booth style seating.

Remember the pact. Don't give him anything useful but don't get yourself bound and gagged again either. Stay alert. Look for an opportunity to escape. Get his address. Can't be that hard to find some mail lying around. An address will help me map my way back to the Gargoyles. God knows I don't want them coming here!

Thorn shuddered at the idea of a showdown at Diesel's home. The real possibility of death loomed. As much as she didn't want to be here with Diesel, she wanted violence between the two men even less. No, she'd handle this one on her own, with her wits, her brains, and yes, if it came to it, with her body.

"Want something to drink?" Diesel opened the refrigerator and pulled out a pitcher, holding it aloft in front of his chest. "I'm having iced tea."

"I'll have a Diet Coke."

"Try again. Your choices are Dr. Pepper, tea, milk, water, or juice."

"What kind of juice?" She wasn't normally so ornery, but being kidnapped by a man who had once discarded her like a used tissue didn't exactly earn her gratitude or cooperation.

Diesel didn't take the bait. "Orange."

"Water's fine." She made a deliberate show of ogling his home, a disapproving frown on her lips.

He added a few ice cubes to the glass from the refrigerator's service panel and then moved to the filtered water dispenser.

"No ice," she interjected at the moment most likely to annoy. She bit back a sly smile remembering a story from her childhood by O'Henry called *The Ransom of Red Chief*. Oh, she could so be that little boy who turned out to be a bigger nightmare to his captors than they were to the child's frantic parents. Diesel wouldn't kill her—well, Trey wouldn't, and she had to believe some of the best parts of the boy still lived in the hardened man he showed to the world—but he might pack her up in the car and dump her off at a neutral spot. If she played her cards right.

Oh yes, there were multiple ways she could handle this herself.

After wordlessly dumping her glass contents out and starting over without so much as a frown, Diesel sauntered over with two beverages in hand. He took the seat opposite her at the table. Strategically, he occupied the spot where he could catch her if she decided to bolt out either side of the booth bench. He slid her water over to her, and she took a sip. The cool liquid soothed her throat and traced a chilling path down her esophagus and into her stomach. More. She chugged the rest down, her body's needs taking over because until that second she hadn't even realized how parched she'd been. With a loud exhale she set the glass down with a bang. Diesel picked it up, refilled it, and returned to his chair.

"Thank you." Thorn took another long series of gulps but stopped midway emptying the glass a second time.

"Now. You asked what happens next." He pierced her with a calculating stare, and for a second, Thorn felt a shiver of nerves. Maybe he wasn't so harmless. But she couldn't allow him to sense her fear, to use it against her, so she made a show of indifference with a roll of her eyes and a shrug of her shoulders.

She ignored Diesel's bait and cast a panoramic gaze through the kitchen, starting on her left. She avoided his gaze by angling the path of her survey over his head to take in the great room with its massive fireplace directly in front of her. An L-shaped sofa defined the outer edges of the space that gave way to a foyer and staircase that presumably led to a second level over the garage. Two side chairs with a small table between them created an intimate nook to the left of the fireplace. Behind the seating area, he'd positioned a pool table.

As far as possible escape routes went, Thorn noted that three windows on the wall to her right looked out into a yard. She'd already logged a door to a deck between the eating area and the kitchen countertop. Like the door between the garage and the house, it, too, had a keypad lock on it, plus a vertical deadbolt. The man valued his security in addition to his privacy.

"Doesn't matter because I don't plan on staying long," she said, locking gazes with him.

"No, you won't be staying long," he agreed far too readily. He leaned back in his chair, arms crossed at his chest. "Not if Spider understands what's at stake."

She didn't like the ominous threat in his words. Was he referring to her or something larger? "I thought the Gargoyles and Heathens had a treaty." At least that's what Spider had told her. Maybe she'd been naive to believe him. Wouldn't be the first time.

Diesel shook his head. "Not anymore." He shifted in his chair and brought both elbows onto the table. "Here's how this is going to go while the negotiations happen. You will obviously stay in my ... protective custody. If you cooperate, you won't be bound. If you keep quiet, you won't be gagged."

Thorn pursed her lips and took in his words. "In addition to wearing a smelly pillowcase over my head, what else does *cooperating* involve?" She made air quotes for emphasis.

A shadow passed over Diesel's features. The scar on the bridge of his nose and above his left eyebrow gave him the look of a world-weary tomcat with the simplest of goals: feeding, fighting, and fucking. Thorn reminded herself that it was possible—not probable—that all the good parts of Trey she had loved were dead.

"Not that," he spat with disgust. "Nobody will touch you. Unlike the Gargoyles, the Heathens aren't rapists nor do they raise a hand to a woman. Ever."

Thorn took in a shallow but shaky breath, unsure of what to say to his passionate outburst. Her lips parted, but no scathing retort came to mind.

"You'll never be alone, but my house is not such a bad prison." The corner of his mouth lifted in a wry half-smile. "Who knows? You might not ever want to leave." And then he laughed and slapped the table.

Thorn smiled at first, his laughter contagious, and then she remembered. She could never trust him, never let her guard down for even a second, because that's all it would take for him to find the tiniest of cracks and crawl back inside her soul.

Chapter Six

Diesel growled, low and deep, from where he sat on the L-shaped sofa catty-corner from her. Thorn had switched the television to some evangelical religious channel, the man on the screen preaching fire and brimstone for sinners who didn't repent. She wasn't actually watching it, was instead flipping the pages of a magazine, but kept a regular rotation between it and any other channels she thought would most annoy Diesel.

Barely an hour earlier, Diesel had exclaimed he'd not even known there was a romance channel until today and prayed to the God of the Religion Channel that he'd never be forced to watch it again after this chapter in the club's history was over. That and Dammit curled up beside her with its head resting on her thigh had been the highlights of her six hours and counting of captivity.

The sun had begun to yield to the shadows as the evening approached. Lunch had been a ham sandwich on stale rye bread with handful of kettle chips. The ancient apple he gave her lacked any sort of tangy juiciness, and texture-wise was more mushroom than fruit. Looking at the bright side, maybe she'd lose a couple of pounds. Her stomach growled in protest.

So far, Diesel hadn't let her out of his sight. He tapped away on his laptop, doing who knows what. He'd taken one phone call but quickly ended it saying he'd send instructions via text. She had no idea how the negotiations were going or even if they had even begun.

At slightly past five o'clock, the doorbell rang, and Diesel jumped to his feet. "Not a word," he warned. As he passed by her, he snatched up the remote, pointed it at the television and cranked up the volume. "Dammit, get down."

The dog tilted a sad-eyed face his way but

slithered to the ground and sat on its haunches between the sofa and oversized coffee table.

"Hold!" he told the dog.

Dammit whined but shifted its attention to her. It crowded closer, and to her shock, the mutt opened its jaws and lightly bit down on her ankle, not hard enough to hurt or break the skin, but not letting go either.

"Silence!" Diesel repeated. The doorbell rang a second time. To Thorn he said, "If you make any noise, she'll bite harder. If you try to move, she'll bite harder, only it won't just be your ankle. Got it?"

Thorn nodded, still in shock that the sweet, gentle hound she thought she'd won over remained more loyal to its owner and had been trained to behave aggressively on command.

Diesel jogged toward the foyer. Thorn's view of the front door was blocked by the staircase. She had no idea if Diesel's visitor was friend or foe, expected or unexpected. Maybe it was some of the Gargoyles who'd found Diesel's home and were there to take her home, though she doubted they'd announce their arrival by politely ringing the doorbell.

A few seconds later Diesel and another Heathen, one of the guys she remembered from earlier that morning, entered the room. The other man carried several bags of something that smelled delicious. Scents of sesame and garlic drifted her way. Had to be Chinese. She loved Chinese food and knew Trey—Diesel—did, too. But she also loved Italian, Mexican, and good old American comfort foods. The man carrying the food wore a cut with the Heathens' patch on it. He headed toward the kitchen. Diesel followed but stopped, and pointing the remote at the television, lowered the volume. He tossed the remote on the sofa next to her and told Dammit to "Release." The dog let go of her ankle and jumped back up on the sofa next to her. It then had the gall to present its belly for a scratch, no hard feelings.

Thorn muttered, "Traitor" under her breath but gave the dog what it wanted under Diesel's considering gaze. She hoped she'd be eating soon. Hunger made her weak in many ways.

At the kitchen island, the other man began removing the food containers all proudly labeled "Happy Golden Tent". Thorn's mouth watered. Diesel shifted his attention from her to the kitchen. She rose and started to walk with Diesel toward the food.

"Go sit down. You'll eat when we're done." Diesel narrowed his eyes at her, and after she sat back down, resumed his trip.

The other man—Diesel called him Python— opened up all the containers and unleashed a symphony of heavenly smells. The rich aromas of beef and broccoli, chicken and green beans, Mu Shu pork and fried egg rolls wafted into her nostrils. Thorn's lips thinned into a grim expression she wrestled instead into a display of indifference. But inside she seethed and resumed her plotting to not only escape to but seek vengeance.

****

Ignoring the plate Diesel slid in front of him, Python plunged his fork into the container of Mu Shu pork and stuck it in his mouth. Diesel plucked the container from his hands and dumped a pile on the plate. Even though Diesel practically grew up in the streets, he'd made a point of learning basic etiquette and table manners. Python rolled his eyes and continued to shovel food into his mouth. Diesel served himself, and his eyes tipped to his view of the next room before he started eating. From his vantage, he could only see her legs, crossed at the ankle, resting on his coffee table. The way her foot fidgeted nervously, he figured her mind was racing to devise a way out.

"What's the update?" he asked. "Hold on." Diesel stood and strode to the living room. Scooping the remote from the table he tapped the volume a few times so the sound blared through the room. He caught a glimpse of her scowl as he returned to the kitchen, remote in his possession once again. He waved his hand, signaling Python to continue.

"Cops came to the shop. Said they were following up on kidnapping accusations. Didn't find anything and left." Python shrugged.

"Hear anything from Spider?"

Python shook his head. "Nothing yet. What you doing 'bout her?"

"She stays here until Spider makes a move. You bring the stuff?"

Python grunted affirmatively.

"My drill is in the garage."

Python snatched an eggroll from the table as he stood and sauntered to the door.

Diesel pushed his untouched plate away. "You hungry?" he called out over the din of the television. Her foot stopped for a moment before resuming its rapid beat. "Whatever Dammit doesn't get will go down the garbage disposal unless you claim it soon. I don't do leftovers."

Her foot stopped again, and she dragged both from the table to the floor waking Dammit from her slumber. Thorn followed Dammit into the kitchen. A wet snout nudged his leg, and Diesel scratched Dammit behind her ear as Thorn entered the kitchen.

"Sit," he said. Dammit was the only one to comply.

"Don't boss me around like your dog."

His back pressed against the chair and exhaustion hung over his eyes. "You want to eat or what?"

She yanked the chair out and sat while surveying the open cartons. He handed her a clean dish, and she carefully spooned a selection of each onto her plate. She took a bite and nodded to his untouched dish. "You don't like Chinese?"

"Not hungry."

"What's the matter? You scared because Spider's threatened to kill you for what you've done? I know you were talking about him. I heard you say his name even over the television."

The legs of his chair screeched on the floor as he stood. "Spider hasn't made contact. Maybe we did him a solid. Maybe he's happy to get rid of you. He sure as hell isn't itching to get you back."

He watched her throat work a hard swallow before raising a napkin to her lips. She wiped her mouth with deliberate strokes, allowing an uncomfortable amount of time to pass before saying, "You're lying."

He scraped his plate into Dammit's dog dish. "Wish I was."

And he did. At least there would be a plan. Spider was supposed to make demands, and there'd be a negotiation to release Thorn. The sooner he got her out of his house the better. However, there wasn't any other place to keep her, not that he'd trust. Damn Spider for being an even bigger piece of shit than he'd previously known him to be. Python lumbered past with his drill and a bag from the home improvement store. "You know which room," Diesel mumbled to him while cocking his head toward the stairs.

Thorn played with the food on her plate. She opened her mouth to speak as a whirring sound floated down from the second floor. She narrowed her eyes. "What's he doing?"

"Installing a lock on your door. And before you

accuse me of treating you like my dog, I'm not. Dammit has free rein of the house."

A flash of challenge shot through her eyes. "You're not locking me in a room."

Diesel dropped his plate into the sink. "I am, and I will. Unless you'd like to sleep in my bed." He strode to her chair and held her chin between his thumb and index finger forcing her face upward to meet his stare. "How 'bout it, Thorn? For old times." He couldn't help himself. Being around her did fucked up things to his body. Her flesh burned in his palm, and all he wanted to do was to claim her mouth, her tits, her everything.

The challenge returned to her eyes and glowed bright. "Go fuck yourself," she spat.

"I see you two are getting along," Python chuckled as he entered the kitchen. "Lock's installed." He tossed a shiny brass key to Diesel. "So, we're even now?"

Diesel stepped away from Thorn and slid the key into his jeans pocket. "You think a split lip and locksmith service makes up for this clusterfuck?"

"How about I take this juicy piece of ass off your hands? She can stay at my place."

As much as Diesel wanted her out of his life, he could only imagine Thorn's fate if she was left alone with Python. There was no way he was letting her out of his sight. He jerked his head toward the door. "Call me when you hear from Spider."

Thorn's shoulders dropped when the front door closed.

"I told you I'd keep you safe. I'm not happy about you being here, but I'm not about to send you off with Python or anyone else. Finish eating," he said quietly and patted his thigh, signaling Dammit to follow him to the living room.

"Trey," she called. His chest squeezed at the

sound of his real name. He stopped.

"Spider really hasn't tried to get me back yet? You weren't lying?"

"Hurry up. I want to go to bed," he grumbled, his back still to her, afraid he'd give away the angry fire seething in his stomach. Anger toward the undercover operation that was dragging on way too long and making him look like a fool, anger toward his club officers and his friends, for putting him in his present situation, anger for the innocence sitting at his table tempting his cock so much that he had to make himself a world class asshole so she'd despise him more. But what made him most furious was Spider's silence. If Cathy were his, he'd be a raging animal, ready to destroy anyone who got in his way to get her back.

Chapter Seven

After two days of no word from Spider, Thorn's mood turned from cranky to world class bitch. Diesel struggled with sending her back to the Gargoyles or fucking her brains out. She barely spoke to him, and the only time a scowl wasn't plastered on her face was when she played with Dammit. In fact, his ugly mutt took such a liking to Thorn, Diesel was convinced Dammit preferred their houseguest over him. But she wasn't a houseguest. She was his captive. That fact smacked him in the face as he locked her in the guest bedroom at night.

"I'm really getting tired of this," she said as he walked her toward her sleeping quarters.

"The ball's in your boyfriend's court." Diesel pushed open the door and flipped the light switch. He hid his smile when his gaze landed on the perfectly made bed, the sheet and blanket turned down like a five-star hotel's. Even in the middle of chaos she still did routine things like make her bed. It was typical for a foster kid to make things as normal as possible.

"Are you sure he even knows you kidnapped me? Maybe he thinks I ran off and he's out looking for me."

"I'm sure your friend Lucy filled him in."

She rubbed her eyes. "*If* you actually let her go."

"Believe me. My guys couldn't wait to send her back."

She dropped her head and her voice and added, "Yeah. She must've told him then."

Diesel leaned on the wall as she moved to the foot of the bed where Dammit effortlessly jumped up and curled into a circle on one corner of the mattress. "Why would you run off anyway?"

"I wouldn't."

"Then why'd you suggest that's what Spider might

think?"

"No reason. Just leave me alone," she said and waved him off.

"Come on, girl." Diesel patted his thigh signaling Dammit, who wouldn't budge from her spot on the bed. "Damn it, Dammit. Come!" The pooch opened her eyes for a moment before letting out an audible sigh and rolling onto her back. "Mind if she sleeps in here tonight?"

Thorn turned her back to Diesel and shook her head. He pulled the door closed when a whimper caught his attention. He left the door open a crack and watched her stroke Dammit as her back shook. She was crying. His forehead hit the door, deciding his next move.

Just lock the fucking door and go to bed. His gaze tipped to her again. "Fuck," he mumbled and pushed the door open. "Are you crying?"

Her back straightened. "No." She sounded like a petulant teenager. "I don't cry."

"Turn around."

She swiped the back of her hand over her cheeks before she turned. "I'm not sad, if that's what you think."

He studied her red-rimmed eyes. "Then why are you crying?"

Her gaze narrowed as she stood. "Because I'm fucking pissed. I'm pissed at you for keeping me here. I'm pissed at Spider for not giving a shit. Both of you can go to hell! I can take care of myself." She didn't bother wiping the tears streaming down her face.

"I know you can. You always were able to take care of yourself."

"Then why don't you do what you did all those years ago, Trey? Why don't you just go?"

He knew there was so much more behind her words. Questions. Accusations. Hurt. Anger.

"I had no choice but to leave you then, and I have no choice but to keep you here now," he said evenly.

She strode to him, her eyes wild with intensity. "No choice, my ass. You're a coward and a bully. That's why you left then, and it's why you're keeping me here now."

He wanted to lash out and set her straight, wanted to shake her into understanding why he did what he did then and now. But, God, he couldn't. What would be the point of undoing so much hard work and suffering? But his pride couldn't let it go, not completely. "You don't know me at all, Cathy. Not then. Not now."

Rage flared in her eyes. "Once, I thought you loved me, and I trusted you. I offered you all that I had, and you greedily took it, took everything, including my fucking virginity and then—poof!—you left. Got what you wanted and tossed me away like a used tissue."

She was poking too close to his rawest of nerves. "Yeah, well you didn't boo-hoo too long over me before you jumped into bed with the first dick that came along."

Thorn flinched, the tiniest of movements, but he caught it and her wrist before her hand made contact with his cheek. He drew in a deep, calming breath. "I think we've both made our points."

She pulled her hand from his grasp and waved toward the door. "Go. Just go."

He watched as she sat on the bed next to Dammit. She tucked her knees to her chest and hugged her legs just like she used to do when they stayed up talking long into the night about their dreams and plans for the future. He strode to the door. He yearned to soothe her like the old days, say, "*I did love you, Cath*", but truth was his weakness where Cathy was concerned. Now was not the time to be weak. Saying the words aloud wouldn't do either of them any good. Not then. Not now. He left without turning around.

****

Locked in a fucking bedroom for another night. They'd turned it into a prison. That sniveling rat, Python, had not only put a lock on the door but he'd nailed a piece of plywood over the window. Heaven forbid if there were a fire. Death would take her in the smoke and flames.

She had no tools to lever up the board. Everything had been removed from the room but a mattress and sheets, a pillow and a Polartec blanket. The mattress was made of memory foam—no coils to bust out and use either as a weapon or a tool. As maddening as being imprisoned was, nothing compared to the humiliation of Spider and the other Gargoyles abandoning her to a man who clearly had no use for her other than as a bargaining chip. Diesel hadn't banked on how little value she had. Neither had she.

This would be her third night in the hellhole. At least tonight she had Dammit for company. She reached over and scratched the pooch's head. "How does he do it, girl?" Dammit cocked her head, ears pricked up. "You know what I mean. How does he get away with treating you like shit while not making you flat out hate his guts?" Dammit gave a woof, a quick muffled sound too soft to alert anyone to danger but loud enough for Thorn to get the message—"Speak for yourself, human." Thorn sighed with resignation.

She needed a shower and clean clothes. Her head itched. Her pits had a clammy feel to them and were probably approaching offensive. How much longer would he keep her here? What exactly did he want the Gargoyles to do to get her back, and what had triggered her kidnapping in the first place? What kind of gang war had been sparked? How serious was it?

NON-RETURNABLE

And what about Spider? What was he up to? She'd overheard Diesel say no one had heard from him or any of the Gargoyles yet, like she'd been written off as non-recoverable or not worth the effort. A sick feeling unfurled in her stomach. This wouldn't be the first time no one claimed her, that she'd been passed over as more trouble than she was worth. She'd lived through too many short-lived periods of raised hopes that were subsequently dashed. People could be so cruel. One family didn't want her because her curly hair and dusky skin made her look "too black" and what did they know about raising a black child, while another family thought her lighter skin gave her cause to have a superiority complex. She never understood why she had to choose between being black or white when she was both. The Rayburns thought she was so quiet she was on the autistic spectrum and God help them, they had "enough of their own problems without having to cater to a special needs child". Her "smart mouth" had gotten her ejected from the Campisi home. Mrs. Bunch thought Mr. Bunch had taken an unhealthy interest in her and dubbed her "Lolita". Oh, not to her face, of course not, because she as only twelve at the time, but she'd heard it nevertheless. Trey had had to explain the meaning to her, much to her mortification. However, that rejection she hadn't minded so much because Mr. Bunch gave off a smarmy vibe.

The closest she'd ever had to a family had been with Spider and his parents. Though they had dangled the hope of adoption in front of her for two years, it never happened. The Emerson home had been her final stop in the foster care system. Spider's mother, Lana, pushed for the adoption, but his father, Grant, had more reasons than Lana for not moving forward. What a world-shattering conversation to overhear late one night when her thirst for a glass of water sent her creeping past their bedroom door just in time to overhear her name. Even now the memory of pausing and leaning an ear toward the cracked open door to hear the rest remained fresh in her memory. Probably because it was burned into her brain, the final brand of rejection. She could still smell the stench.

"What about Cathy?" Lana had said.

"What about her?" had been Grant's reply.

"We can't just up and move away and leave her behind."

"We can after she turns eighteen. She's not our responsibility anymore when that date comes."

"Grant," Lana's voice pleaded softly. "How can you be so heartless? She's family now."

"She's trouble, Lana. There's a reason she's been in the foster system so long, passed from family to family."

Thorn clenched her eyes closed and willed away the memory that ended with her fleeing, tears streaming down her face, back to her room where she kept a stash of hidden snacks to soothe the angst in her heart and gut. That was exactly how she felt now. Even Spider had had enough of her. Poor, fat, unwanted Cathy.

Well fuck them! Fuck them all! As soon as she got out of here, things were going to change. The only person she could count on was herself.

She had to escape. There had to be a way.

What could she do?

She sat heavily on the turned down bed and fingered the linens. Diesel had good taste. They had to be at least 500 thread count, tightly woven with paper thin threads. She could floss her teeth with these sheets. She could...

Wait a second. What if she slipped the edge of the

sheet between the plywood and the window and braced her feet against the wall?

****

Hours later, Thorn never thought she'd be grateful for the few extra pounds she carried on her frame but that night she thanked her lucky stars for them. After three hours of sawing the hemmed edge of the flat sheet between the plywood and the wall, she had finally, finally begun to pry the nails out of the window frame. Had she been sure she was alone in the house and not worried about loud noises alerting her captor, she probably could have done it in thirty minutes. Thorn hadn't been blessed with much patience and she'd stretched her meager endowment to its breaking point, but it had been enough. By about one o'clock in the morning the fourth and final nail pulled free from the upper windowsill. God bless Python for being a lazy ass and only using one nail per corner.

That was when finesse mattered most. The plywood was heavy and awkward, but Thorn had wisely planned ahead. The thirty minutes she'd spent maneuvering the bed into place below the window had been time well spent because the mattress muffled the sounds of the board and her tumbling backwards when the last nail finally yielded to her efforts. Dammit hadn't even lifted her head, had only cocked an ear to the side.

"At last," Thorn whispered as she gave a fist pump into the air to her canine audience.

Now to inspect the window itself. Most windows were installed to keep intruders out, not keep home owners in. She hoped she only needed to slide it open, kick out the screen and bars, if there were any, and slip out onto the roof overhanging the back patio. She'd worry about the drop from the second floor to the ground later. How high could it be if she first dangled by her hands from the gutter?

The latches turned easily, and the window slid open without even a scrape.

So far so good.

The lawn shimmered where the full moon reflected on the accumulated dew. She could do this. *Ha! Take that, asshole.* Diesel had forgotten she was no stranger to sneaking out at night. Many a time the pair of them sat out on the roof of the foster home they shared, smoking a stolen cigarette and dreaming about life. All she'd ever wanted was a family. Not money, not fancy clothes or cars, not fame. She thought she'd found it with Trey. Wrong. She thought she'd finally found it with the Emersons. Wrong again, other than Teddy. Teddy Emerson hadn't let her down, although he wasn't Teddy anymore but Spider. She kind of missed Teddy, but Teddy wouldn't have given her a family like Spider had. They were two different men. The Emersons had sent Teddy away to military school hoping to curb his aggressive tendencies. Spider had returned in his place, and that's when they'd become lovers. Spider and the Gargoyles were her home, her family now.

Thorn shook the memories from her head and slipped her right then left leg through the window, pausing on the windowsill. She stole a glance back into her prison where Dammit sat alert on her haunches watching her every move but not making a sound.

"Good girl," she whispered. "You were the best part of this crappy experience." Dammit whined and stood up on her legs. That was the nudge she needed to shift her ass forward and her weight onto the roof. She slid the window shut to keep Dammit from trying to follow her but also to prevent any changes in pressure from rattling the bedroom door. The dog jumped on the bed and pressed its nose to the glass, watching Thorn's every move. She put a finger to her lips silently begging the dog to keep her secret, turned and began her escape.

The shingles were a little slick beneath her bare feet. Oh yes, barefooted had always been the best way slip away unnoticed, though she had her shoes tucked into the waistband of her pants. For later. For when she hit the road, maybe hitchhiked, to where she wasn't sure yet.

At the roof's edge, she used a support beam to slow her drop to the ground some ten feet or more. Though tempted to put her shoes on and walk through the sound-muffling grass—soiling them with a misstep in Dammit's shit would not be fun. Barefoot across the pavement it would have to be until she escaped Diesel's yard.

She looked into the windows of the main floor of Diesel's home. The oven's night light shone, but otherwise the main area was dark. The room next door, the master suite, however, was illuminated. She could see Diesel's bed, still made, but the man himself was out of sight. *He's probably in the bathroom. Get going, girl. Now!*

Tiptoeing probably wasn't necessary, but Thorn wasn't taking any chances. She moved quickly past Diesel's bedroom and around to the side of the house where she assumed she'd find a gated exit. Wrong. Nothing but a continuation of the six-foot high wooden fence with no space between it and the house that was large enough for her (or Dammit for that matter) to squeeze through. *The gate must be on the other side.*

She retraced her steps and approached the master suite window again, crouching down as she'd done before. Nothing about the still life had changed. Ditto for the kitchen. She continued around the back deck to the opposite end of the house where there had to be a gate or opening in the high wooden fence.

If the roof outside her prison had extended around to the front of the house she would have avoided the backyard altogether, but that hadn't been the case. The backyard had been her only option, but she'd be damned if she let a fence prevent her from escaping. She'd find something to help her scale the damn thing if necessary.

She never had to confront that reality because no sooner had she turned the corner when she found her path blocked by a shadowy pillar. A large, angry pillar that shined a flashlight in her eyes and said, "Trouble sleeping?"

NON-RETURNABLE

Chapter Eight

Strands of hair stuck to Thorn's sweat-stained cheeks. It was as if all of the air had left her body like a discarded balloon. If Diesel wasn't so fucking pissed off, he'd almost feel sorry for her. He had to give her credit, she'd worked long and hard for the two minutes of freedom she thought she'd won. Did she think he was stupid? He had trained himself early on for trouble that happened at night. Darkness brought out the worst in people. He learned that lesson in foster care. Things went bad at night. Men beat their wives at night. Women drank themselves into unconsciousness at night. Kids were abused at night. It was as though darkness hid the ugliness. If one couldn't see it happening, maybe it didn't. His mind played those tricks on him early on until he knew better. It was then he learned the signs shit was going down. The creak of a floorboard, the rustle of bedsheets, the stillness in the air. It always amazed him how much noise someone made when trying to be silent.

Damn, she was beautiful though. And damn if she hadn't haunted him with her presence, arousing feelings he had no business having. She wasn't his, never would be. He only wished his dick could understand that.

Thorn's feet stayed planted on the ground as he steadied the flashlight toward her face and he stepped forward. "Funny, I couldn't sleep either. Not with all the racket going on in your room. Took you long enough. It was at least a couple hours ago since you pulled the first nail out." He tipped the light down her arm. "Ripped up your hands, too." He grabbed her wrist and lifted her right hand to get a better look. Swollen and bloodied lines decorated her fingers and thumb.

She pulled her hand back as though she'd touched hot coals. "Don't put your hands on me," she spat. Hatred shone through her eyes as she shot daggers at him through the misty darkness.

"What was your plan, Thorn? Once you got out of the yard, where were you going? Not like Spider wants you back."

She took a step forward tipped her face to meet his. "You're all the same. You think women are property to be owned."

"If you think that you don't know me at all."

"No? You're keeping me hostage in your house. What am I supposed to think? You turned into a monster." She stepped back. "Maybe you were one all along, but I was too stupid to see it until now."

His pulse beat in his ears, and he grabbed her hand squeezing her fingers together. She whimpered and clenched her teeth but maintained her cold stare. Diesel pulled her closer. The heat of her body ghosted over his as their breath came hard and fast. He pushed her back, sandwiching her between the house and his body. Rage clouded his eyes. "You're right. I'm a fucking monster. I don't give a shit about anyone, especially you."

A small sob escaped her lips, and his mind raced back to a time he found her alone in a bedroom of the foster home they shared. He wished he could pull her into his arms and kiss her wounds and disappointments away like he did all those years ago.

She swiped away a tear with the pad of her finger, leaving a smudge of dirt on her cheek. "Don't you dare think I'm crying for you. I'm done shedding tears for you, Trey. You don't deserve them."

He pulled back his fist and rammed it through a house shingle a foot away from her face. He couldn't help it. He needed to punch something. He needed to feel physical pain to transfer the focus from the jagged blade turning in his chest. He swallowed hard. "You're right again, Thorn. I don't." Exhaustion melted over his body. "Let's go." He said softly grabbing her arm and nudging her toward the back door. She didn't put up a fight. Instead her shoulders slumped in defeat, and she allowed him to lead her inside.

Loosening his grip on her arm, he led her to the stairs, flipping light switches off as they walked through the first floor. Dammit's whimpers filled his ears as they trudged up the stairs. Diesel unlocked the guest room door and Dammit bounded out, almost knocking them both over.

"It's okay, girl." Diesel scratched behind Dammit's ear as he surveyed the room. Leaving Thorn and Dammit in the hall, he stepped inside and surveyed the window before stooping down to pick up the ruined material. "These were good sheets," he mumbled.

Dragging the tattered fabric behind him, he led Thorn back downstairs to the master suite. "Lay down," he said waving his hand toward his bed.

Thorn whipped her head around. "W-what?"

"You heard me. Lay on the bed." He grabbed her arm once more and pulled her to the side of the bed. "Put your hands together."

"Why?"

"Jesus, Thorn. I'm tired. You're tired. This is going to happen so just do what I say."

Her hands shook as she brought them together. He ripped a strip from the sheet and wrapped it around her wrist a few times before tying a tight knot.

"Now lay down and put your hands over your head."

"I'm not about to lay down and let you rape me." Her voice cracked.

Diesel closed his eyes and shook his head wondering what had happened to them. There was a time he thought they'd be together forever. That was before life, and clubs, and others stood in their way. Now she was afraid he was going to tear her clothes off and rape her.

"Believe it or not, women *want* to sleep with me. I don't have to rape anyone. I just want to get some sleep, and this is the only way that's going to happen right now."

He opened his eyes and found her studying his face. He guessed she was deciding whether to believe him. Finally, she sat on the edge of the bed and pulled her legs onto the mattress highlighting more bloodied lacerations on her knees and shins. "Arms up." He tied the loose end of the makeshift rope to the headboard. "That should do it. Please don't try any more escape moves for the next few hours."

He turned to walk away.

"Where are you going?"

"Over here." He cleared the book he'd been reading from the small sofa in the corner and set it on the end table. After draping the tattered remains of the sheet over the sofa and throw pillow, he switched off the reading lamp.

"Maybe I'm not the monster you think I am," he said into the darkness as he stretched out his long frame on the too small to be comfortable makeshift bed.

****

"Wake up, Sleeping Beauty."

Thorn squinted as Diesel yanked the blinds open, flooding the room with sunlight. Pins and needles ran through her arms when she rolled her wrists above her head. "Yeah, I'm sure I'm a real beauty right now." She was nose level to her armpits, and she was sure there was more oil in her hair than in Spider's hog. Talk about a hot mess.

Moving to her side, Diesel reached over her body to cut her wrists loose with his pocketknife. A wave of his musky scent filled her nostrils in a good way. His heat singed her belly. "Fresh towels are in the bathroom. Help yourself to anything you want in there," he said helping her up.

"My punishment for trying to escape is a shower?"

He held her gaze for a moment. "I guess so." He shrugged and stepped to the dresser. She watched as Diesel rummaged through the drawers and dropped a pile of clothes at the foot of the bed. "It's the best I can do," he said before leaving her in his bedroom untethered and unguarded.

Thorn glanced out the window to the patio beneath the overhang that had served as her thwarted escape route. Every muscle in her body protested the thought of trying it again. Stabs of throbbing pain poked at her limbs. She didn't have the energy to bolt. Even if she did, there was no doubt Diesel would be on her heels. A hot shower was a hell of a lot more appealing. She trudged to the bathroom, shedding her clothes along the way.

Diesel's bathroom was the complete opposite of what she'd expected. Fluffy towels were neatly folded on a shelf like the ones she'd seen in the one fancy hotel Spider took her to in Vegas soon after they started dating. She turned the knob and ran her hand through the water streaming from the oversize shower head until the temperature was as hot as she could handle. She stepped out of her panties and into the walk-in shower. Closing her eyes, she tipped her face up and allowed the water to wash over her skin. She flipped open a bottle of high-end shampoo. She wondered if he'd lied about having a woman in his life. In her admittedly limited experience, men like Diesel didn't care about their grooming products.

After washing her hair, Thorn stepped out and grabbed his razor from the sink and shaved her legs and armpits. She grinned evilly at the thought of Diesel using a dulled razor to bloody effect. It would serve him right. She felt human again, and for that she wouldn't apologize.

Before she finished she gave her bra and panties a quick wash and hung them on the towel bar to dry. Her fingers were like prunes when she finally twisted the knob to the off position. She wrapped one fluffy towel around her body and another to squeeze the excess water from her hair. She raked her fingers through the damp corkscrew-like curls, watching them bounce over her shoulders. Spider liked her hair straight, and she spent at least a couple hours daily fighting her natural curls with a hot flat iron. She tugged one of the curls at her cheek and watched it spring back. "Curly hair, don't care," she muttered recalling the hashtag she'd seen on social media.

Thorn padded into the bedroom half expecting Diesel to be waiting for her. Instead her nose picked up the delectable scent of bacon setting off a deep growl in her belly. She grabbed a pair of gray sweatpants from the pile Diesel left on the bed. Her only pair of panties were drying in the bathroom.

"Guess I'm going commando." She stepped into the pants, and the loose material skimmed her bare mound and teased at the flesh of her ass as she moved. She smirked as she picked through the selection of t-shirts he left, each one was decorated with a Heathen MC logo. She chose the black one emblazoned with day glow green "HEATHEN" in bold letters. Pulling it over her head, she imagined it must've fit snugly around Diesel's chest since her ample breasts strained the fabric. For a moment she considered searching his closet for a loose hoody to hide her curves, but the mouthwatering lure of bacon overruled her decision.

She crossed her arms at her chest as the delicious aroma called her to the kitchen.

"It's about time. I was about to send the search and rescue crew to find you." Diesel threw a strip of bacon in the air, which Dammit deftly caught, munched, and swallowed in seconds.

"It was good to take a shower." She cleared her throat. "Thank you." She almost held back the last words, but somehow, they felt right.

"Hungry?"

Her gaze traveled to the pans filled with scrambled eggs, bacon, and sausage on the stove. "Starving."

"Sit." He jerked his head toward the kitchen table and pulled a plate from a cabinet. In a matter of seconds, she sat before a breakfast feast.

She picked up her fork and poked at the eggs. "Is this some kind of a trick? You put something in these?" She squinted at the plate.

Diesel huffed a chuckle. "I haven't drugged your eggs. Eat them before they get cold."

Her stomach rumbled again. She was so hungry she'd take her chances. Swallowing the first small bite, she didn't taste anything out of the ordinary. In fact, the flavor was extraordinary. The eggs were on the dry side, just as she liked them. She nibbled on a slice of bacon. The savory crispness was heaven.

Diesel briefly disappeared before returning with a first aid kit he set on the table. He took the seat next to her and said, "I would have done this last night if I'd known how bad those cuts and scrapes were. Not to mention I was so fucking tired." Flipping open the kit, he pulled out a few alcohol swabs, ointment, and bandages. "Let me see your hand."

Extending her free hand, she watched him examine the wounds on one hand while she continued eating with the other. "Why are you being so nice all of a sudden?"

He shrugged off her question keeping his focus on her injuries.

"I mean, it's not like I've been all that nice to you." He touched an alcohol pad to a gash on her finger. "Ouch!"

She watched as he pursed his lips together and blew on the cut, sending a shiver through her body that settled low in her belly. He dabbed ointment on a bandage and wrapped it around her finger.

"And why should you? You were kidnapped and kept against your will for reasons that have nothing to do with you except for who you're with. I'd be pissed, too." He worked on the remaining wounds on her left hand and then gestured for her right. She set her fork down and turned her chair toward him to give him access to her other hand. Her knee brushed against his as she extended her palm. "You know, I didn't want this either. I didn't ask my men to kidnap the Gargoyles' old ladies. I wanted to settle this turf war Spider created in a civilized way. I'm not sure he's capable of it though." He systematically dabbed at and blew on the angry scrapes on her hand, bandaging the deeper cuts. "What do you think is the answer?" Finally, he lifted his dark-eyed gaze to hers.

"You're asking me what you should do about Spider and the Gargoyles?" Spider had never consulted her on club business. Ever.

He moved his gaze from her hand to capture her stare. "Yeah. That's exactly what I'm asking."

"I—I don't know. Spider is so … angry. He's not one for talking things out or compromising. It's not who he is."

Diesel rose, the legs of his chair scraped along the floor. His shadow fell over her as he stood close enough to touch her but didn't move.

"Oh wow, forget about my hand. Look at yours. That's from when you punched the wall last night," she said as her gaze hit the raw and swollen knuckles of his right hand

"It's nothing."

She held his fingertips and took a closer look. "No, this is something. Sit." Sliding the first aid kit around, she patted the table for his hand as he sat back down. "Looks like you reopened a wound. Have a habit of punching things?"

"Only since you popped back in my life."

She shot him a smile and a shake of her head as she ripped open an alcohol pad. "This may sting," she said and tapped the pad gauze on each knuckle. Just like he'd done for her, she blew softly over his skin after each dab.

He winced. "You know when you came out in my baggy sweatpants with your crazy curly hair, you brought me back to when it was us against the world."

Her gaze lifted to meet his, and her mind raced back to a time when she, too, thought it was them against the world. "You used to say that all the time and I believed it. Until…" Her voice trailed off. What was she going to say? *Until you left my heart in shattered pieces with a family that didn't care?* There was no use in bringing it up again. She shook her head and finished bandaging the last knuckle. "Never mind. There. Best I can do. Try not to punch anything for a couple days." She grabbed her plate and carried it to the sink. Being so

73

close to him, taking in his scent, touching his skin—it was all too much, especially when Dr. Jekyll stepped in to replace Mr. Hyde.

"Why are you with Spider?" he asked.

She turned on the water and rinsed her dish, fighting back the lump in her throat and the tears barely held in check. The scrape of his chair sounded, and she sensed his body was close.

"Why?" His husky voice blanketed her ear.

"Don't," she whispered as the first tear escaped and rolled down.

He spun her around, caging her between his arms. "Do you love him or do you stay because you're scared?"

"Please. I can't talk about this, not with you of all people." She pushed against his arm, but he wouldn't budge. "Why are you doing this?"

He cupped her face in his hand, forcing her to meet his sharp gaze giving her a window to the rage and lust that were seconds away from combustion. "You tormented me last night. Being in the same room and listening to you while you slept … it took me back to the basement we used to go to get away from our shitty lives. But as crappy as our lives were, we had each other. That night you gave yourself to me has taunted me in my dreams for years. It's always the same, I can feel you, taste you, hear you like you're there with me. It's so fucking real." His breath was heavy on her lips. "But last night you were right there, but you weren't because you're not mine and it rips me apart."

Cathy closed her eyes, and the scene was vivid under her lids. She also kept it alive. As painful as it was, it was one of the only times she'd ever felt truly loved. Until…

Her eyes flew open. "Rips you apart? What the hell do you think it did to me when you left, Trey? When you said all those terrible things to me? It destroyed me," she whispered, and God, yes it wrecked her. But right then with Trey's body against her and his breath ghosting over her face, she wanted him more than she'd ever wanted anything in her life.

"We both have deep scars, and I'm sorry I was the one who gave you yours. But that was in the past. I know I have no rights to you, but I need to know why you're with him."

"It's not a simple answer."

"Do you love him?"

"I—I..." Her answer trailed off. She couldn't get her mouth to say the words. "I can't talk about this."

"You don't have to say anything," he whispered.

It was far too easy to get sucked into Trey, like she was starving, and Trey was a delicious seven course meal. She leaned into him like it was the most natural thing beside breathing. Even though she was on the larger side—at least that's what Spider said—she fit against the contours of his body like she was made to be there, just like she remembered. Her breasts pressed against his chest, her mouth a whisper away from his.

He brushed his lips over hers, testing her desire, which ignited the fire growing deep within her core. She teased him with a nibble to his bottom lip, inciting a deep groan as he encircled his hands around her waist and lifted her to the counter as if she were weightless. His tongue invaded her mouth and his hands snaked up her shirt, palming her breasts and pinching her nipples. She wrapped her legs around his waist. Even through the barriers of her sweatpants and his jeans she felt his steely erection as he ground against her pussy. Her flesh was on fire as he trailed his tongue down the hollow of her throat and lifted her shirt, freeing her generous breasts. She leaned back on her elbow and watched his talented tongue possess her nipples, sucking each one into his mouth and laving them into taut peaks. She dragged her fingers over his shoulder to the back of his neck and through his hair as his mouth did wicked things to her body. He pulled her closer with one palm under her ass and the other slipping under the baggy sweatpants and between her legs.

"You're so wet for me." His raspy voice vibrated through her as he touched her so gently she wanted to cry. Or maybe it was the whole fucked up situation that brought tears to her eyes. God, she wanted him more than she'd ever wanted anything, and even though it felt so natural, so *right*, she knew it wasn't. Not like this. Not when she belonged to another man.

"Trey..." Thorn hardly recognized her own voice, let alone the voice coming from the next room.

"Yo, Diesel! Where are ya?"

"God damn it," Diesel hissed and pulled Thorn from the countertop. She righted her shirt seconds before Python rushed into the kitchen.

Python's stare bounced from Diesel to Thorn. "What the hell, Diesel?"

"What the hell? You broke into my house. How'd you get in here?"

Python narrowed his eyes. "You gave me a key. Remember? I banged on the door so hard I almost knocked it down. But by the looks of things, you were doing some banging of your own." He jerked his head toward Thorn.

Diesel stepped in front of Thorn blocking Python's view. "What the fuck are you doing here?"

"I tried to call you, man. The cops arrested the biker who pushed drugs on that girl who OD'd. Just like you thought. It was a Gargoyle."

Chapter Nine

A wave of tension rolled from Diesel's shoulders. The arrest would at least keep the Heathens from under the microscope. Maybe it would also speed up the undercover operation.

"Who was arrested?" Thorn asked.

Diesel turned toward her and by the looks of her knitted eyebrows it appeared the tension that melted off him shifted to her. He knew she wondered if it was Spider sitting behind bars.

"Some dude that goes by Dirt. Fitting don't ya think?" Python barked out a laugh.

"You know him?" Diesel asked her.

Thorn nodded. "He's one of the newer members. Got fully patched last summer with a group of younger guys. I knew there was something about them I didn't like."

"Like what?"

"They're a cocky group. I mean even more cocky than all you bikers. But that wasn't all. The new guys act like they rule the place. I've noticed Spider gives them a lot of leeway for newbies."

"Think they have something over Spider?"

Thorn seemed to disappear within her thoughts for a second before shaking her head slowly. "No. Couldn't be."

"What is it?" Diesel asked.

Her gaze shifted from Diesel to Python. "Nothing. It's nothing."

"If there's something we should know, girl. You better spit it out," Python demanded.

"There's nothing you need to know. Why should I tell you anyway? I'm a Gargoyle. I'm not about to divulge my club's business to a Heathen!"

Python lifted his brows and tipped his chin at her shirt. "You're a Gargoyle, huh? Looks to me like you're playing both sides. Careful, old lady, that's a dangerous game."

"I'm not playing anything," Thorn said quietly.

Diesel studied the worry on her face. She knew something, and he needed to find out what it was.

Python's laser gaze sliced through him. "Can I talk to you? Alone?" Diesel nodded and led him to the front door. They stepped outside. "What the fuck is going on between you and Spider's old lady?"

"There's nothing going on. But she's got information we need."

"Bullshit. I walked in on something cooking in the kitchen and it wasn't food. And why the hell is she wearing a Heathens shirt?"

"It's not what you think." But it was *exactly* what Python thought. Diesel rubbed a palm across his forehead. "Look. Stay outside and call Flint. Have him bring the members in for an emergency meeting. I'm gonna find out what she knows."

Python huffed out a breath. "Hurry up."

Diesel nodded and slapped Python on the shoulder before going back inside the house.

The sound of running water greeted him as he stepped into the kitchen to find Thorn doing the dishes. It was like the past smacked him across the cheek with an open hand. The last time he'd seen Cathy she was doing dishes in the foster home they shared, the day before his eighteenth birthday. She'd already known he was leaving, and he knew washing dishes was something she did to keep her hands moving, when she was upset, when she tried to swallow her feelings. He remembered calling out, "I'm packed," as he held his beaten up duffel bag in one hand and the parting gift from the foster family—a couple of twenties—in the other. She'd continued with her chore. The only indication she heard him was a slight shrug of her shoulders. "Cath…" The rest of his words had swum in his throat refusing to be heard. He couldn't take back the harsh words he'd said and tell her how he really felt because he knew she'd never let him leave without her if they were a couple, if she were older. He had no choice but to turn and go, which made him both a hero and a coward.

As the years passed, he tried to convince himself he was a hero for being unselfish enough to give her a chance at adoption, but as time went by, he wondered if he'd made the right decision. And leaving her with the lie that she would have only tied him down, that he never cared about her, had haunted him every day since.

Diesel didn't know how long he stood in the kitchen doorway watching her as memories of that day rammed through his head until she turned and shot him a worried glance. She pushed the faucet lever down with her wrist and ripped a paper towel from the spool. "He gone?"

"No, but still outside. You don't have to do the dishes, you know." He flipped his index finger toward the sink.

"Just keeping busy. I have a bad feeling about all this."

"Wanna talk about it?" He posed the question in a casual way as if it didn't matter if she chose to open up or not. But in reality, he needed information, and she was his only source.

"I shouldn't. I mean, I'm not even sure of it." She wadded the paper towel into a ball, squeezing it into her fist.

Diesel pulled a stool out from under the counter and patted the seat before taking the one next to it. With her feet still planted next to the sink, she seemed to be fighting an internal battle. He didn't speak, knowing that pushing her would only make her retreat.

Finally, she took the seat he offered. "I know I shouldn't be telling you this, but…" She paused, closed her eyes and bowed her head. After a second ticked by, she clenched her fists and pounded her thighs. Her hazel eyes met his and held them. "That girl who lost her life? More will die if something's not done."

"Done about what, Cathy?" he asked quietly, as though his normal volume would make her stop talking.

"The drugs. I doubt that was a one-off thing. I think the Gargoyles have turned to pushing drugs on teens as a source of income, and I think they're using, too."

"Spider?"

She hesitated and then nodded. "The morning your guys took Lucy and me, I found a syringe in the garbage bin at our condo. Well, that and a thong that wasn't mine." She exhaled slowly. "One of those things didn't surprise me too much. The syringe though? That was the first time I'd seen anything like it in our home or anywhere else on Gargoyle property."

Diesel hands curled into fists. "Did you ask him about it?"

Thorn shook her head. "I went to the clubhouse to talk to Lucy first. He doesn't know I found it."

"Besides the syringe, why do you think Spider's using?"

Thorn rested her forearms on the counter and interlaced her fingers together. She took a deep breath, keeping her eyes forward avoiding his stare. "He's had really crazy mood swings lately. I've been trying to stay out of his way ever since the last bad one when…" Her gaze fell to her hands. "Well, it was a bad one."

"God damn it, Cathy. Did he hit you?" Dammit whined at Diesel's feet and sat up with her ears back like she did the last time she ate one of his shoes. Smartest fuckin' bad dog on the planet.

"Yeah. Clocked me a good one on the jaw. He was all sorry about it later. Said he was under a lot of pressure." She pulled her shoulders back, took a deep breath, and let it out slowly. "We'd had plenty of fights— bad ones—but he'd never laid a hand on me before. Never."

Diesel slammed his fist on the counter. "I'm gonna kill him."

Her palm rested on his forearm. "No. You're not. This is why I didn't want to tell you. Violence isn't going to stop him, and it's not going to stop them from pushing drugs on teens. I think the drugs are coming from the new members the Gargoyles inducted."

"Dirt?"

"Him and his friends who joined at the same time. Spider lets them do whatever they want. I asked him about it once, and he said they're bringing in a lot of business so he gives them a lot of leeway. Maybe I'm naive, but I never thought it was drugs, but now that I think back, and knowing they arrested Dirt, it's all coming together. Spider's been so erratic and paranoid since the explosion at the Titans' clubhouse in Chicago a couple months ago."

Diesel recalled the event. No one was hurt, but the word was the Titans were convinced the package bomb was sent as a warning from a rival MC club. The bomb exploded shortly after delivery but before anyone could get close enough to open it. No one was hurt, but the Titans' clubhouse was badly damaged. The news made all of the Midwest MC clubs jumpy for a while, wondering who did it and why and if it was going to happen again.

He ran a palm over his face. "This has become more than a turf war around stolen cars," he said absently.

Diesel took her hand. There was something he had to know before moving forward with his plan. "Thank you for telling me, but I need to know where your head is, Cath. Despite what you've shared, if your loyalty still lies with Spider and the Gargoyles, I'll let you go, right now, back up whatever escape story you want to tell. But if not, if you give your word you're not playing both sides here, I could use your help."

Python's words rang in his head. He couldn't afford to put his club in danger because of his feelings for her.

Her gaze bounced from their joined hands to his face. "Why would you trust me? And for that matter, why should I trust you?"

He huffed out a laugh. "Because inside here," he said tapping his chest, "we're still Trey and Cathy, even though I'm a dumbass for not having the balls to tell you how I really felt when I had the chance."

She lifted her brows. "You gonna tell me now, or do I have to wait another ten years?"

Diesel studied her face. She deserved to know. "This is going to sound really bad, and you may not choose to believe it, but I did what I did *because* I loved you."

She pulled her hand away. "You're telling me you said those words back then, that I was just a warm body to fuck and you didn't care about me because *you loved me*?" She huffed, her nose wrinkled, lips curled. "You and I don't have the same definition of that word."

Diesel cringed. It sounded way worse out loud. "You still had a chance at being adopted. It was your chance to have a real family. I had nothing to give you. Nothing. You still had another two years in the system."

"Oh yeah. That really worked out for me. You didn't want me. After you left, I was transferred to another foster home." Tears welled in her eyes, but she blinked them back and swallowed hard. "No one wanted me. No one. Not even you. I was all alone, Trey. I aged out of the system just like you did only I had another two fucking, shitty years to do it without you. Do you understand that? You were the only real thing I had— thought I had—and you shucked me off too, just like the Simpsons, the Rayburns, the Campisis, the Bunches, and God, even the motherfucking Emersons!"

He sucked a strangled breath of air into his lungs. "I'm sorry." The words sounded lame, and he wished he could take them back as they left his mouth.

Her eyes widened. "You're sorry? That's the best you got?" She jerked her gaze away saying, "Shit!"

He opened his mouth to say something. He wasn't sure what. The urgent pounding at the door kept him out of the hole he'd dug.

****

Thorn released a long slow breath when Diesel left to answer the door, relieved to have a short reprieve to digest what Diesel had just served up. He said he was sorry. He said he loved her. *What the ever-loving fuck?* She had spent the past ten years thinking he had moved on and never looked back, barely given her a second thought beyond being a notch on his bedpost, some pathetic girl he used to know. He'd seemed unfazed even by her sleeping with a rival club leader. She had hated him for his indifference. That had been the cruelest cut.

"Where is she?" A shrill voice rang out.

"Lucy?" The chair slammed to the floor as she ran out of the kitchen and through the family room to the front door.

"How'd you find out where I live?" Diesel asked.

"I followed your guy. Python, is it? You should think about giving him another ration of the few brain cells you Heathens share. He's as dumb as a flat tire."

"Hey!" Python's footsteps clomped through the kitchen. "Who the fuck? Oh shit, it's you," he said, glaring at Lucy. "What are you—like some stray cat we can't get rid of? You weren't supposed to come back."

She threw him daggers with her eyes and turned to Thorn. "Are you okay, darlin'? Are you hurt? Did they do anything to you?" She threw her arms around Thorn and murmured in her ear, "And why the fuck are you wearing a Heathens shirt? Have you lost your fucking mind or have they brainwashed you?"

Thorn pulled back and said, "I'm okay. Really." Her chest swelled with warmth. At least someone was worried about her.

Lucy grabbed her fingers. "Then why do you look like you've been giving a hand job to a pricker bush?"

Thorn tugged her hands from Lucy's grasp. "It's a long story, but, girl, are you insane? You shouldn't have come here! Did you come here alone?"

"God, I hoped they were keeping you somewhere other than the clubhouse. Spider has lost his mind." She narrowed her eyes and captured Thorn's gaze. "It's bad, Thorn. Really bad. It's Chicago times a thousand."

Chapter Ten

Diesel pulled his cell from his back pocket, gazed at then tapped the screen and held it to his ear. "Flint? No, I haven't checked my phone in a while. What's up?"

The color drained from Diesel's face as he stood in front of Thorn. He lowered his cell and tapped the screen again, motioning for Python to move closer. With his caller on speaker he asked, "Python's here with me. Repeat what you just said, but slowly for us this time."

A man's voice boomed out of Diesel's phone saying, "The Gargoyles got explosives into the clubhouse somehow. Several of our guys are inside. Spider sent a text to you and me claiming responsibility and that you gotta call him."

Thorn's mouth fell open, and she shifted her wide-eyed gaze to Lucy, who could only nod solemnly to confirm her fears.

The Heathens' clubhouse? Where Lucy would have told them I was being held after they released her?

Thorn twisted the hem of her Heathens' t-shirt as she contemplated the possibility that Spider hadn't cared one iota if she was injured or even killed in his plot. Maybe that was part of his overall plan. Her shoulders dropped from the weight of this new development on top of the days of silence that had passed since her kidnapping.

Python frowned and said, "He's bluffing. And even if he isn't, why can't our guys sneak out the back to get away from the bomb?"

Flint's growl rumbled over the speakerphone. "The backdoor? Well, fuck me, Python, why didn't I think of that? No, asshole. They can't evacuate the clubhouse. No one goes in or gets out. In addition to the package bombs inside, they've got tripwires installed around the doors and windows. Pitfall confirmed it. Cut or tug on the wires and the bombs will go off."

Thorn knew Spider had made bombs before, learned by starting with smaller, harmless versions that exploded in clouds of flour or gym chalk dust. If the gossip she'd overheard from a couple of the other old ladies were true, Spider had been behind the explosion that damaged the clubhouse of the Titans in Chicago. Not wanting to stir up trouble in his own backyard, the Gargoyles had supposedly traveled west to Chicago where no one would think to blame a Detroit MC. It might have been a tall tale the other ladies tittered over, but Thorn knew better and so did Lucy. This Heathen booby-trap was something she knew Spider was not only capable of, but he'd relish doing, and in the most ruthless manner possible.

Diesel shifted the phone to his other hand. "Who else is inside, Flint?"

"Pitfall. Opal. Ranger. Ranger's old lady, Diamond, and that new Heather, Blue."

Thorn grimaced at the mention of the Heathers. She knew what they were without even being told. The Gargoyles had their "Bunnies", a candy-coated term for women angling to become a club member's old lady. In theory being an old lady was supposed to mean a committed and monogamous relationship, but none of the women were stupid enough to expect fidelity. The Bunnies and Heathers had to endure a gauntlet of sexual demands from any or multiple club members. She'd walked in on more than one tryst, supposedly never more than a harmless blowjob, according to Spider. "What's the big deal?" he used to say. "It's not like we fuck 'em."

Only that wasn't true either. She wondered if Diesel lived by the same loose code of ethics and fidelity rules as Spider and his gang. Her heart told her "no", but her head told her not to be a fool, that this was life in a club. An MC woman's role included looking the other way in private, putting her foot down for show in public. They all accepted that as part of what they'd signed up for.

Flint's voice shifted into a hushed and worried tone saying, "What do ya want me to do, Deez? I feel like a bag of popcorn in the microwave ready to explode."

Diesel's jaw tightened. "Tell me more about the packages inside. Where are they? What do we know about them?"

"Pitfall said they were delivered early, around nine this morning. During Python's watch."

"Right." Diesel swung his attention to his other club brother, fury etched into the grim set of his mouth and jaw. "When I say we're on high alert, that means you watch the fucking club; you watch out for each other. You sure as fuck don't let some rival club casually deliver a fucking bomb!"

Python raised both hands. "It wasn't that way at all. Calm down a second and let me—"

"I'm not going to calm the fuck down! Not while our brothers and old ladies are being threatened! I want answers!"

Looking cowed, Python continued to move his hands in a placating motion. "Okay, okay. Here's what must have happened. As I was leaving to come here to tell you about the Gargoyle arrest—because you weren't answering your phone—a delivery guy rolled up with a bunch of boxes. I thought they were tools and small parts. That's what the boxes said on the outside. I signed for them, opened the garage door, and told the guy to unload them inside. I yelled for Pitfall to open and inventory everything, and then I headed over here. I didn't know what they were!"

Flint chimed in. "Diesel, Spider somehow knew the second Pitfall opened those boxes because his text arrived right as Pitfall was calling. Pitfall knew something was off, and when he couldn't reach you, he called me."

Python pointed to Lucy and said, "Or, maybe this one knows more than she's letting on. Why was she watching our club? So she could follow me? Maybe so she could tell Spider when to send that text."

Lucy charged into Python's space, yelling, "I had nothing to do with the bombs, but when I heard Spider bragging about his plan, I figured you Heathens would be swarming to some other location! Wasn't all that hard to spot your Heathens jacket zooming north—"

"So you followed me so you could send me a Christmas card? Fuck that story, lady!"

"So I could find Thorn, you dumbass!"

"Shut up, both of you, so I can think." Diesel spun toward Lucy, his eyes narrowed, head cocked slightly to the side. "Hold on. Earlier you said this was Chicago times one thousand? Are you talking about the package bomb sent to the Titans' clubhouse? Spider was responsible for it?"

Lucy squared her shoulders and raised her brows, not backing down to either Heathen. "I didn't say that. My concern has always been Thorn."

"You might not have said it, but that's what you meant, didn't you?" Diesel stepped in front of Lucy, closing the gap between them.

Thorn pushed them apart, wedging into the narrow space between them. "Stop it! The Titans don't matter right now, but Spider's current plot does. He will detonate a bomb if he's planted one, and I believe he has."

"Thorn," Lucy warned in a hushed voice.

"We're talking about people's lives, Luce." She turned to Diesel. "Spider never copped to planting the Titans' bomb, but I'd bet money on it. He's built smaller, harmless ones before. He found directions on the dark web and had been experimenting."

"Flint, get over to my place as quick as you can."

"Already on my way."

"Where are the other A-teamers, Speed and Breakneck?"

"They left two days ago for Milwaukee by way of Windsor. The idiot delivery driver drove into Windsor, Ontario, and got stuck in customs. Long story. That's all you even wanna know. Somebody had to go get the goods unstuck and delivered."

"So you're telling me that other than yourself, the only officers or A-team members who aren't in danger of being blown up are standing in this room or are off in Canada?" Diesel's jaw clenched when he finished, but otherwise his body language showed no signs of the fury that drove his earlier outburst. Just like the Trey she remembered from her teen years. The boy who never cried, hardly ever lost his temper, but when he did, watch out. He was like a revving car with one foot pressing the accelerator while the other firmly pressed on the brakes. His brake foot rarely wavered, but when it did, his lapse was explosive but brief.

"Breakneck and Speed are on their way back from Milwaukee, but won't be here until tonight," Flint said.

"Ride safe but ride fast." Diesel ended the call and then a few taps later appeared to be reading something on the screen, probably Spider's text. Thorn watched as he stared at the screen. A second, two seconds ticked by in silence before he put the phone back down on the counter. He began to pace the room, his hand rubbing the back of his neck. "I still don't understand how Spider or his club members could slip past everyone and put trip wires around all the doors and windows and no one sees them doing it?"

Thorn's gaze darted between Python and Diesel, but she didn't move a muscle, didn't even take a breath.

"Must have been when we were sleeping, I guess."

"You guess?"

Python widened his eyes and shrugged, but otherwise seemed to shoulder none of the blame Diesel cast at his feet. Despite his earlier outburst, Diesel was far calmer than Spider would have been if the tables were turned. But then again, their personalities were so different. Diesel usually held his cards close to his chest about almost everything. Most of the time Spider was unapologetically transparent because he didn't care if you knew his plots or what you thought of them. However, if Spider didn't want her to know what he was up to, he could be amazingly unreadable. From experience, she knew whatever he'd been cooking in his closed pot mind was something she wouldn't have wanted the burden of knowing about. Like the Titans bombing. He never actually told her he was behind it, but she pieced enough clues together to realize he was, clues he selectively doled out because he was also a very proud man.

Diesel focused on some far away object while he thought.

"So, what's the plan 'til then, Diesel?" Python asked. He had taken a seat on the sofa and spread both arms out along the tops of the back cushions. He slouched low and rocked his knees together and apart while his gaze wandered the room.

A stab of annoyance curled Thorn's lips into a

sneer. Typical sniveling coward, only wanted to dump his problems off but had no solutions to offer. If this was one of the Heathens' best, the Gargoyles would chew them up and spit them out. She'd seen Spider and the boys do it before to at least three upstart clubs that tried to form and claim territory in the Detroit suburbs. None of them had lasted more than a few months.

"I'm thinking." Diesel's pacing moved him closer to where Thorn had taken a barstool seat at the kitchen's island.

She could make the choice for him, provide him the solution he needed, but part of her wanted, no needed, to know where she stood with him after what had happened a few minutes earlier. She was very sure where she stood with Spider—forgotten, written off, maybe even being set up as an example. But with Diesel? Part of her recited that old adage, "Fool me once, shame on you. Fool me twice, shame on me." Had she been a convenient temptation or were her and Diesel's fragile, shallow roots forever entwined? Her heart said the latter was hers and Diesel's truth, but her head warned her not to be so foolish. Not again. Not ever again.

Diesel stood beside her and caught her gaze, a wide array of unreadable thoughts flickering across his face. Her heart tried to convince her that this beautiful, damaged man might put on a brave show, but he wasn't that different from the fourteen-year-old boy she first met and fell in love with. But while she could see the truth, she wasn't so sure he could or ever would.

She understood what she needed to do. Thorn drew in a slow deep breath and said, "You want a bloodless end to this ridiculous eye for an eye standoff? Well, then this is what's going to happen next."

****

"You don't call the shots around here," Python

spat.

"Shut up, Python," Diesel warned.

"Apparently neither do you, slime-ball. Let her talk," Lucy said.

"I know what you need to do," Thorn repeated, her voice flat and empty of emotion.

Python stood and sauntered toward Thorn, towering over her and glowering. "I'll just bet you do, don'tcha, Honey Pot."

Diesel growled a warning to his Sergeant-at-Arms. He wasn't having any intimidation or threats cast Thorn's way. She hadn't asked to be kidnapped and thrown into this turf battle as a pawn. None of this had been his idea either. A couple of hotheaded Heathens had caused this. They had dragged the conflict into the mud of cheap shots and outrageous one-upping. Lives were at risk. How had everything gone so wrong?

Thorn crossed her arms and glared at Python. "You talk to me like that one more time and I will rip off your balls and stuff them in your fat gob."

Python puffed up his chest and leaned closer to Thorn. "Sure you will, sweetheart. And I'm all trembly afraid of a couple of old ladies from a rival club. Who you wag your fat ass at and fuck don't make you anyone special. Every two-bit hooker has figured that out by her second day mattress surfing." He pointed at her and took a step back. "You remember that."

Diesel's left fist crashed into Python's jaw and sent him crashing to the floor.

The decked man groaned and pushed up on one elbow, the other wiping blood off his lips. "Jesus Christ, Diesel! Why'd you hit me?"

"You act like a dog, you stay down like a dog until you can show some fucking respect, asshole!" Though his knuckles still stung he clenched and unclenched his fists. Good thing he'd used his left. Now he had a matched pair of split knuckles. Diesel rarely lost his temper, but when he did, it felt like he'd been sitting on a pile of dynamite.

Python spat a spray of blood onto his kitchen floor. "Shit, Diesel. This bitch is Spider's old lady, who I caught you with one hand down her pants and the other one up her shirt when I walked in. You think that's gonna help our case? And now you wanna act like some kind of white knight? You've lost your fucking mind! Heathens before Gargoyles, or did you forget that once your cock rose up?"

Lucy groaned and unleashed a scowl on Thorn. "Oh, Thorn, honey. We gotta get you outta here."

Every word out of Python's mouth was like a drop of acid. Diesel may have lost focus for a moment—Python was right about that—but he was dead wrong about Cathy. She might be Thorn to Spider and the rest of the Gargoyles, but she was his Cathy first and always would be whether she or Python or Spider or anyone else realized it or not.

"You're one stupid son of a bitch, but you're right about one thing. Now's not the time to fight with each other. Spider and the Gargoyles are the enemy." Diesel extended a hand to Python to help him to his feet.

Thorn, who had been watching the argument in silence, turned to face him straight on. "You two done with your pissing contest and ready to hear my idea?"

Python insinuated himself into the space between Diesel and Thorn. "Please tell me you ain't gonna listen to anything she's got to say. Her loyalty is to the Gargoyles, not with us."

Diesel ignored Python and said to Thorn, "I'm listening. Talk."

Chapter Eleven

"You're going to do a trade. Me for your guys. You'll let me go in exchange for Spider defusing the bombs."

She forced herself to keep eye contact with Diesel as his questioning gaze searched her eyes. "Is that really what you want?" he finally asked.

"Of course that's what she wants! You two can end this right now! That's what everybody wants!" Lucy spouted. "I'm calling Dagger now and will let him know. Shit, he's going to be pissed off that I came over here." Lucy pulled her phone from her purse and stepped outside. "Hey, babe," was all Thorn heard before she shut the door.

Diesel nodded at Python. "Give us a minute."

Python grumbled something about being dumped in the garage like a bag of trash as he shuffled back to the kitchen and slammed the garage door.

"Don't do this because you're afraid. I can take care of Spider." His voice softened. "I can take care of you, if you'll let me."

His last words floated over her like the scent of warm biscuits. It was like home. A real home. Not one fabricated on lies and false club loyalties. She closed her eyes, holding the feeling of Trey one last time before making the break. Her lids opened, and she pinned him with an icy stare. "I don't need you to take care of me. I belong to Spider and the Gargoyles. He's the one who's been there for me, not you."

Diesel grabbed her shoulder. "He treats you like shit."

She shrugged. "He loves me." Even as the words left her mouth, she knew they weren't true. Spider didn't love her. In fact, she wondered if he'd even go for the deal. But she also knew his pride would get in the way. He couldn't pass up an opportunity to look like a hero to the club. He'd make a big show about getting her back and how much he sacrificed to do it. Of course, Diesel would come off looking like a fool as the leader of the club that tried and failed to force the Gargoyles to do something she still wasn't sure she understood.

"Do you love him, Cath?" Diesel's thumb caressed her shoulder so lightly, she almost didn't feel it.

The tenderness in his touch sliced through her, and she bit the inside of her mouth to keep from screaming "no". But what she wanted didn't matter. The only way to stop Spider was to give him what he wanted—to one up the Heathens at their own game and yeah, maybe get her back at least for appearance's sake. However, Spider's apparent willingness to treat her as collateral damage greatly diminished her value in the transaction she was proposing.

Did she love Spider? Had she ever loved Spider, or had it been because he and the club offered her what Diesel wouldn't? Only one answer would move her plan forward. She sucked back a sob and swallowed. "Yeah. Yeah, I do."

A wisp of emotion floated over Diesel's eyes, but it was gone in a heartbeat. If she had blinked, she would've missed it.

Lucy pushed open the door, and her gaze landed on Diesel's hand on Thorn's shoulder. "Oh, for God's sake, cut that out! Thorn, don't listen to him and his lies! He kidnapped you, remember? Remember who you are!"

"He was just apologizing. None of this was his fault. It wasn't his idea to kidnap me."

"Bullshit. He's president of the club, Thorn. He's responsible for his men. In my book he's mostly to blame."

Diesel dropped his hand from her shoulder. "She's right. The club comes first. My allegiance belongs to the Heathens, and yours—Thorn—belongs to the Gargoyles, if like you say, you truly love Spider." He leveled an icy glance at Thorn. She'd gotten used to him using her real name over the past few days, but just like his gaze, her club name from his lips sent a shiver through her.

Thorn made no further comment as Lucy guided her to the sofa. "Give us some privacy, would ya?" Lucy barked.

Diesel stepped to the door and punched a code into a keypad on the wall and a beep sounded. "I'll be in the kitchen. Don't do anything stupid. I need her to ensure the safety of my club."

A pawn. That's all I am to him. A lump swelled in Thorn's throat, and she inwardly cursed at herself for holding a thread of hope there was something more between them.

"Okay, love. I talked to Dagger and he talked to Spider. This is what's gonna happen—"

Thorn raised her palm. "Hold on. What did Spider say?"

"What do you mean?"

"You know what I mean, Luce. Is he relieved I'm okay, that I'm not in the Heathens' clubhouse? Is he happy he's getting me back? Does he want me back?" God, she hated how her words sounded. Desperate. Needy. Powerless.

"What kind of fucking questions are those? Of course he wants you back."

"But why? Because he'll look like a hero to the rest of the club for recapturing his property? Or because he wants *me*? I need to know."

"Look. I know things haven't been the greatest between you two, but you're the prez's old lady. You're in the ultimate position. Do you know how many girls would give their left tit to be you? You have to overlook certain things—we all do—it comes with the territory. You know that," Lucy said in an urgent whisper.

She knew Lucy was trying to carry her to the top of her Gargoyle old lady pillar, but Thorn still felt like old scraps thrown into the dumpster. "I shouldn't have to overlook *things*."

Lucy craned her head toward the kitchen. Diesel watched them closely as he leaned against the counter with his arms crossed. She turned back to Thorn. "This is not the place to hash this out. Let's get you back home and we'll talk. You and I. Maybe there's a way to make it better. I need to get you outta here. I can tell he's messing with your head."

Thorn caught Diesel's stare. A silent showdown zipped through the space between them before Thorn lowered her gaze. "Okay. Tell me the plan."

****

He tried hard not to believe it, but Diesel finally pounded into his own dumb head that Cathy wanted to leave him and go back to Spider and that he had no choice but to agree. Her eyes said it all.

But it hurt. Dear God, it hurt—the dashed hopes of discovering the difference between a mirage and a bleak reality, the hopelessness of realizing that he and Cathy were irreparably broken, the agony of ripping off a bandage he'd worn for so long but finding the flesh beneath putrid. The truth was she didn't want him, not anymore. She wanted to go back to Spider. That was the deepest, cruelest cut.

The irony was once upon a time he had been the noble one to walk away so she could have the family she always wanted. Turned out the Gargoyles were her family.

She'd chosen family over him.

Wasn't that what he'd given her all those years ago? He couldn't take it back now.

In the end, he had to let her go and return his focus to the safety and welfare of his club.

Lucy left first after she served as the middleman in the negotiations with Spider. Diesel was sure Spider wasn't showing his full hand, but neither was Diesel. Once the plan was set, Thorn, Python, and Diesel drove toward the rendezvous point in his Dodge Charger to the sounds of Python's out-of-tune humming of some stupid earworm song. The song had played earlier on his car radio before he turned off the entire sound system in disgust.

Thorn gazed out the window. She'd cried saying goodbye to Dammit. *Shit.* She was still fucking crying. She loved that stupid dog more than him. What an idiot he'd been. He should have marched her ass right back to the Gargoyles as soon as he discovered what his misguided brothers had done. He should have—

"For fuck's sake, would you stop humming that godawful song, Python!" Thorn cried in a stuffy sounding voice.

Python did as he was told, and the car fell into a thick and ponderous silence as they rolled down the highway.

"Pull over," Cathy said so quietly, Diesel wasn't completely sure that was what she said.

"What?" he asked.

She turned to him. "I said pull over." Her voice was stronger that time. His eyes tipped to hers for a second before he slowed and came to a stop at the side of the road. He threw the gearshift into park and turned toward Cathy, meeting her gaze.

"What the fuck?" Python barked from the

backseat.

"Turn around, Python," Cathy demanded.

"Jeezus. Deez?"

"Do what she says," Diesel answered without taking his eyes from hers.

Python muttered something inaudible and the leather seat popped as he moved.

Cathy cupped her hand against Diesel's cheek, her touch electric on his skin as her palm slid to his shirt. Her fingers curled around the fabric and pulled him closer, their mouths so close her breath coated his lips. He hands itched to touch her, but he didn't dare because he'd never be able to let her go. Her lips pressed to his, and caution was tossed out the window into the highway tumbling freely among the passing cars. Her hair tangled in his fist as he deepened the kiss, branding the memory into his brain—her taste, the feel of her tongue on his, her soft whimper—he needed to remember it all. She pulled back breathlessly breaking the connection. Her swollen lips parted like she was about to say something.

"Don't," he said. He didn't want to hear any sorry-ass explanation of why she picked Spider over him and he sure as shit didn't want to hear her say good-bye. Diesel pulled his hands from her like she was a hot pipe on his bike. With one hand gripping the gearshift and the other on the wheel, he slammed on the gas and continued their course to give Cathy what she wanted and in return saving his club brothers.

As they neared the meeting spot next door to the Heathen's clubhouse, Diesel caught sight of three hogs parked in front of the pawn shop abandoned during the last recession. The "For Rent" sign in the front window had yellowed, its edges curled and the once black ink faded to gray. Spider stood at the apex of the pyramid of Gargoyles, watching them drive into the parking lot.

"Who are the other two men with Spider?" Diesel asked.

"That's PeeWee on the left and Dagger on the right," she said evenly.

Diesel stopped about twenty feet away from the trio of men and put the car in park. He turned to Python in the back seat and said, "Come take the driver's seat. Leave the engine running and haul ass out of here if anything bad goes down." He turned to Thorn. "You ready to go home?"

She blinked those hazel-green eyes that could always pierce through his bullshit. Her tears were gone. Guess that meant she was indeed ready to leave him, maybe even choking back a few tears of joy and holding her smiles in check. "I don't want anyone to get hurt," she said somberly.

Too late, Cathy. He nodded and took in a deep breath. "No. Can't have that."

Diesel checked his watch. The plan he'd negotiated with Spider was uncomplicated and straightforward—give Thorn back to the Gargoyles in exchange for the disarming and removal of the bombs. The only problem with that plan was that they ended up worse than they were before all the kidnapping nonsense began. Damn those assholes for being such hotheads and jumping the gun when they took Thorn and Lucy. He still hadn't fully dealt with that situation, a complication to the problem of the Gargoyles encroaching on the Heathens' territory and the drug deals going down and dirtying up their town.

If only his club had been more patient, trusted that he had a plan. Well, guess what, Heathens? He still had a plan, and though it wasn't going to play out as he'd originally intended, sometimes a man had to regroup. And sometimes he couldn't trust anyone but himself to ensure there were no further complications.

****

Thorn weighed how she needed to play her role in this negotiation. If Spider thought for even a second that she'd fallen for Diesel, she'd be out on her ass and God only knows what other punishments the other club members might want to dole out. When Lucy had handled the negotiation, she had listened in. Spider's voice had been clipped and void of emotion. He'd never once asked to speak to her or inquired about how she was. Nothing. It played out like a business deal. Had Spider already written her off? His chill reaction to Diesel's demands surprised her. She hadn't expected him to quickly and easily agree to the terms of the deal—her for the disarming of the Heathens' clubhouse. That wasn't the Spider she knew. She expected him to throw in more demands. Something else was going to go down. She could feel it in her bones. Or maybe he had been bluffing about the bombs all along.

How should she play her role? Spitting mad at Spider for having had to wait so long for any action to recover her? Traumatized by her kidnapping ordeal— locked up, no food, no access to clean clothes or a bath for days on end? All true … mostly. Taunting of Diesel for ultimately gambling on a bad move that cost him more than he gained?

And where did that leave her with Diesel? The chances of her being able to pick up where she left off with Spider were slim to none. That was less due to Spider's wishes than her own. The odds of Diesel wanting her? No point in pondering it. She didn't want any bloodshed, however, and that was why she'd play the role needed to minimize any chance of that happening.

"You can't trust Spider or the other guys. Stay on your guard," she murmured to Diesel right before he jerked her forward by the arm, a bit of theatrics they'd agreed to earlier.

"I never have before. Don't see that changing anytime soon," he muttered.

Spider's expression gave away nothing. In all Thorn's years together with Spider since their late teens, she had never been able to find his tell. She wasn't the only one, and if his lover couldn't crack his secrets, who could? Spider was an outstanding poker player for the same reason, and the rest of the guys talked about him like he was some kind of legend for his infamous ability to bluff.

"Thorn. You're looking a little worse for wear," Spider drawled in that lazy way he had when he was setting up a dramatic moment.

"So are you, Spider. I gather you finally got around to missing me?" Bitterness tinged her tone. She couldn't help it. Days had passed with no word from him. Sure, he'd been playing some kind of game of chicken, but she didn't appreciate being his pawn any more than she appreciated being drugged and hauled out of the clubhouse like a sack of potatoes.

Spider lifted a single brow in a sardonic salute. "Cried myself to sleep every night wondering how … I might get you back." The corners of his lips curled up, not quite a smile, not quite a smirk.

Diesel stopped the pair of them about five feet away from Spider, who stood flanked by PeeWee and Dagger. "As we discussed—Thorn for my people. How are you going to disarm the bombs you planted?" he asked.

Spider chuckled and reached inside his shirt pocket. He pulled out an older styled cell phone and tossed it at Diesel, who deftly snatched it out the air before it could strike him in the head. "That's your antidote."

"My antidote?" Diesel turned the phone over in his palm but kept his gaze on Spider. "It's not disarmed yet?"

"No, sir. That's up to you. Here's the code. You ready? Your memory good enough or do you want to get a paper and pen to write it down." He crossed his arms at his chest. "I'll wait."

"Before I do, answer me two questions—" Diesel began.

Spider gave a mock bowing of his head. "If the knowledge is harmless to my club, then certainly."

"You have anything to do with the Titans' explosion?"

A flicker of smile passed over Spider's lips. "What's the second question?"

Diesel released Thorn's arm' and she took a spot catty corner from each of the two men squaring off. Her gaze ping-ponged between them. Spider was doing his typical double-talk so far, but though he might not have a tell, he did have a habit of bragging. The boasts would come, eventually.

"The second question is about some shit I been hearing about some new street drugs, supposedly a synthetic fentanyl mail-ordered from China and cut with street grade heroin. You know anything about that?"

Spider sighed and glanced back at PeeWee and Dagger in turn, as if giving them some sort of signal. Thorn's muscles tensed in a fight or flight reaction. He *was* planning something. There was an air of fuckery oozing from his every pore. "You should be thanking me for handicapping the Titans. They were getting too strong. I…" He paused and raised a finger before proceeding. "*Someone* protected you and yours as much as they did me and mine. Maybe we both should be grateful for that at least."

Diesel nodded. "And the drugs? One of your guys was picked up for pushing at the high school. You know anything about that?"

Spider's gaze locked with Thorn's. She'd asked him this question before and he'd always denied any involvement with drugs, and she'd believed him, until she found the contents of their bathroom wastebasket. He owed Diesel no explanation. Thorn knew what was coming next—an outright denial that would be a lie.

"Yeah, so what? In case you hadn't noticed, things ain't been so good since the recession. A club's gotta do what it must to survive. Detroit's a tough town."

Thorn gasped. "Spider! You promised me."

Spider kept his face toward Diesel but cut his eyes to the side to meet her gaze. "Not your business, Thorn, so shut your fucking mouth."

"No! I won't!" She parked her fists on her hips. "You agreed. No drugs! You also promised me no Bunnies in our home, certainly not in our bed." She slipped between the two men and squared off with Spider, nearly nose to nose since they were about the same height.

"Watch your mouth and step aside. Me and the boys went to a shitload of trouble to get your ass back, and this is how you speak to me? This is how you thank me?"

PeeWee lunged forward and grabbed Thorn by her arm. "Let go of me!" she screeched and jerked her arm from his grasp.

"Hey!" Diesel narrowed his eyes and glared at PeeWee. Thorn felt a momentary triumph. It buoyed her spirits … until she caught Spider's all out scowl.

"Ain't this cute, a Heathen sticking up for a Gargoyle old lady. Makes me think you didn't treat my

Thorn here like the lady she is," Spider said with a lift of his chin. Sarcasm rolled off every syllable.

Thorn's pulse began to gallop. She couldn't be the focus or the deal would go off the rails. "It wasn't the Taj Mahal, but they didn't hurt me, Spider."

"I wasn't implying you were hurt or *forced* to do anything," Spider mocked. "I know you two have a history. Lived in the same house for a while. I always told you not to trust anyone."

Her and Diesel's past had come out a long time ago when she and Lucy were talking about the clubs. She never thought the information would be used against her. "That's ancient history, Spider. We hadn't seen, let alone spoken to, each other in over ten years."

Spider's lips stretched into a smile, but it didn't reach his eyes. Thorn knew she wouldn't have a home to return to if Spider thought she'd been unfaithful to him. The double standards ran deep with the Gargoyles. The Heathens were probably no different. That was one of the downsides of life in the "one percent" as the outlaw clubs were sometimes called.

"Well, Diesel. I'm feeling short-changed here," Spider began, "What else do you have to offer in exchange for the lives of your club members and your clubhouse?"

Thorn's mouth fell open. "He's letting me go, Spider. That's the deal."

Spider cut his eyes in her direction, his message received loud and clear. He didn't want her back. He wasn't here to get her back at all. What was he after instead? Spider returned his attention to Diesel.

"What are you playing at?" Diesel asked, his eyes narrowed.

Spider crossed his arms at his chest and zeroed his gaze on Diesel. "Not playing a game at all. You and I both know this has been a long time coming. I'm tired of getting a fraction of the chop shop market and think it's time I got it all. There just isn't enough for the both of our clubs."

"The Heathens ruled Detroit long before most of your members stopped shitting in their diapers. We let you guys settle into our city. Even gave you a piece of the action so you'd be a first line of defense between us and Chicago, but you shit all over our generosity and got your hands dirty. Pushing drugs on kids? What the fuck is wrong with you, Spider?"

Spider huffed a laugh, "You think I'm gonna let you call the shots? I have to wait for Diesel to give me my allowance? Fuck that. A Gargoyle waits for no one."

Diesel continued, "You owe it to your club to make good on this deal. You're in a ton of shit already with one of your members in jail. Cops must be sniffing around, asking questions, even following you. I wouldn't doubt it if they were watching this whole scene go down now."

Spider laughed. "I can handle them."

Diesel shrugged. "I'm sure you think you can, but if something happens to a Heathen tonight, you better have some clean underwear on because you'll be spending a lot of time at the DPD." Diesel nodded to PeeWee and Dagger. "All of your guys will."

Spider must've bought it because after a glance to his guys he said, "I'll throw you a bone this time and take my old lady back. I did kind of miss having her around." Thorn forced down the bile rising in her throat when his eyes trailed down her body. "The code is 75643292. Punch it into the phone and the bombs will disarm."

"How do I know that you're telling me the truth?" Diesel asked.

"Because I don't want to blow myself up. We're

coming in and taking everything out. Not leaving evidence behind, especially since you're in bed with the PD." He nodded at PeeWee. "Take Thorn back the clubhouse."

Thorn pulled her arm from PeeWee's grip. "I don't need help to walk ten feet." She stole a last glance at Diesel as he punched the code into the phone.

His gaze moved to her as she walked by. "Take care, Cathy."

"Don't address my old lady like that." She heard Spider bark as she slid a helmet on and straddled PeeWee's bike. What she wouldn't give for it to be Diesel's bike and to wrap her arms around his waist and let him take her away. Far away from Spider and the Gargoyles.

"It's her name, asshole," Diesel answered.

She shot Diesel a smile as PeeWee skidded out of the lot.

Chapter Twelve

"I saw you smile at him. You fucking him or something?" Spider had given her a chilly reception from the time he stumbled into the clubhouse with all the boxes taken from the Heathens and the ride back to their condo. She thought she'd be happy to be home, but the place looked different. It felt different.

"That's your answer to everything, isn't it? You think I'm having sex with someone else. Let's deal with the real problem here, Spider." It was always the same fight, and it exhausted her. "If things aren't working between us, let's cut our losses and go our separate ways."

He cocked his head. "You *did* fuck him. While I was bustin' my ass to get you back, you were playing house with a Heathen, weren't you? I'm not so sure you were even kidnapped in the first place. How convenient they let Lucy go but kept you. You still *want* to fuck him!"

"No, I didn't, and no, I don't. Unlike you who is fucking every Bunny in the clubhouse, I don't shit all over our relationship in plain sight while pretending— barely—to be a faithful partner."

"Think what you want, but you can't leave. You're my old lady. You're here for life. After all I've done for you, Thorn, you should be begging for my forgiveness."

"Jesus, Spider. This isn't a life sentence. This is our lives. Don't you want to be with someone who can make you happy?"

Spider laughed. His laughter went on for so long Thorn wondered if there was some joke she was missing. When he finally stopped laughing, he clapped his hands together. "Oh, baby, you never were the sharpest tool in the shed. You think I keep you around because you make me happy?"

Thorn bristled at the insult. This wasn't the first time he'd called her dumb. She had never been a top student, had struggled in school. The teasing and bullying made focusing on her studies even harder. It was a miracle she graduated from high school, but with Trey's help, somehow, she had, barely. She might not be as good of a book learner as Spider, but she wasn't dumb. She learned very quickly by watching. You only had to show Thorn stuff once, and she got it, like cooking or driving directions or people. Her instincts about people were sharp as tacks, and they were telling her now that things could never go back to being how they were before her kidnapping, not after what happened with Trey. He'd stirred up too many emotions that showed her what she might have with the right man. Spider wasn't him and never would be. She deserved better.

"If you aren't happy, why do you stay with me, then?" she asked.

"Believe it or not, Thorn, it's because I know you like the back of my hand. I've known you longer than any of the other Gargoyles. That means I trust you most." He rubbed a hand on the back of his neck and squinted at her. "Though, I'm seeing cracks in your loyalty to me."

Thorn huffed a laugh. Was he serious? "My loyalty to you? You planted a bomb in the Heathens' club house where there was a good possibility I was still being held captive. I think that's shows a pretty serious lack of loyalty."

Spider took two steps closer to her, his gaze boring into hers. "You think I didn't know where you were every second since the Heathens kidnapped you and Lucy? There was no fucking bomb, not a real one anyway, as they'll soon realize. Shit, Thorn, I knew that little prick would eventually take you to his crib and then to his bed. I knew you'd jump at the chance to fuck Diesel again for old times' sake." He rolled his eyes. "You had your romp, but you're now back and you're still mine. You're still my old lady."

Thorn's mouth had dropped open, her brows knitted in disbelief as Spider made their relationship sound more like a master and pet than a partnership between a man and a woman. Hell, Dammit the dog was treated better than she was.

"And what about the drugs?" Thorn asked, trying to keep her voice even and under control. She never got anywhere with emotional accusations. Spider was immune to tears, and she wasn't a fan of them either.

"What drugs?"

"I know, Spider. Don't lie to me. I know the Gargoyles are dealing now."

"Says who?" He smirked at her, a quick lift of his chin, a narrowing of his eyes. He was lying. She knew it. He didn't care if she knew it but obviously got his kicks over playing innocent.

"A young girl died. Word on the street is she was linked to the Gargoyles."

"Word on the street? Oh yeah? Heathens' street maybe. Nobody else is saying that." Spider reached out and tapped the side of her head once, twice. She dodged his third attempt. "I think they been messing with your head. You get kidnapped…" He made finger quotes, clearly being sarcastic. "You don't know up from down anymore. I'm gonna let this go for now because maybe you been traumatized." Spider slipped his finger beneath her chin, lifting her jaw up to close her gaping mouth. "Now that we got that out of the way, the sooner we get back to normal the better. Okay?" He captured her eyes with his, holding them in an unblinking, unforgiving gaze.

Thorn wasn't going to get any answers, not tonight. Best to let the dust settle and try again. Tomorrow. Thorn drew in a long deep breath before nodding slowly. Yes, tomorrow, she'd try again.

Spider dropped his hand back to his side. "I got a lot going on right now and need to work off some stress, and you need to be reinitiated into the Gargoyles. We can kill two birds with one stone. Take off your clothes and get ready for the hardest, roughest fuck of your life. But take a long hot shower first to wash off the Heathens' filth."

****

The pounding, the music, and the whoops of the men should've put Diesel in a good mood, but it had only darkened his temper and amplified his headache. He leaned back in his chair and closed his eyes.

A knock at the door followed by the squeal of the hinges as the door opened. "Yeah, Flint," Diesel said without looking. Flint was the only one who, after a cursory knock, let himself in before being invited to do so and the only one Diesel tolerated it from.

"We got a new Heather ready and willing to be initiated into the club. Want me to send her in?"

"No," Diesel said. The very thought of some random woman sucking him off left him cold.

"No? You not feelin' good? Want a beer? It's good for what ails ya. Get it?"

Diesel huffed out a laugh. Beer was Flint's answer to most troubles and what the amber liquid didn't solve a blowjob usually took care of the rest. Up until a few days ago, Diesel had been a fellow disciple of this philosophy. Things had changed since Thorn had come into his life, bringing Cathy back with her. The realization of what he'd been missing since he said his goodbyes to her all those years ago had smacked him upside the head. What the ever-loving fuck had he been thinking? The only woman who filled his thoughts was Cathy. Her face was the only one he dreamed of seeing in the throes of passion, her cries of pleasure the only music he wanted to hear.

Fucking hell! She was back with Spider, warming his bed, kissing him, fucking him. He couldn't allow his thoughts to wander any further into that treacherous territory. They stabbed at his gut like a knife, twisting and turning until he couldn't bear it. She wasn't his. Not anymore, if she ever was. *Fuck!*

He'd screwed up with her. Again.

Diesel opened his eyes and gazed through Flint at some indeterminate focal point. "Ever wonder why we do what we do?"

"Not sure what you're talking about, boss, but I came in here asking if you wanted to initiate the new Heather. Shit, if I were you my pants would be around my ankles and that girl's lips around my cock by now, not trying to solve the problems of the world. Look, we won the battle. Cops heard everything, thanks to your tipping them off. They'll make their move soon, I'll bet. You deserve to celebrate."

Funny, Diesel didn't feel like celebrating. "We didn't win anything."

"Business is picking up over the past few days. The guys are happy. That's a win in my book. I have just the thing to put a grin on your face. She's a cute little thing. The guys are all panting over her, Opal especially."

"Then let Opal initiate her. I'm not in the mood."

"Not in the..." Flint shook his head and banged the heel of his palm against one ear. "Don't think I heard you right there, boss. Sure sounded like you said you weren't in the mood for a blowjob. You feeling okay?

Not coming down with the flu or some Ebola thing are you?"

Diesel had to chuckle, though it was more of a strangled sounding imitation of the real deal. "I'm sure it's just a passing thing." *No, it's really not.* "I'll leave it to you to bestow the initiation honors upon someone else. I've got some calls to return and some business deals to check on."

"Anything I can help with?" Flint asked.

"Maybe. Some guy named Topper from the Peoria Rebels keeps calling wondering if we want to do business."

Flint pursed his lips and cocked his head, eyes narrowed. "The Rebels? Huh? Really?"

Diesel mimicked Flint's expression, curious now at his lieutenant's reaction. "You know these guys? What kind of business are they in?"

"Can't say I know them, but I'd heard they were in business with the Chicago Titans—cleaning titles, I think—'til those boys lost their clubhouse to the fire. Seems like Spider was courting them hard to joint venture and share Illinois for a small cut of Michigan. Maybe that's not working out so well for them and they're looking for a similar deal with us?" Flint cracked his knuckles, deep in thought, nodding. "You want me to call this Topper guy, see what's what?"

"Yeah, don't make any commitments, just see what they want and why." Diesel leaned back in his chair, his fingers steepled. "I've got a bad feeling about this, like there's something going on we don't know about."

Flint nodded and pulled his phone out of his pocket. "I'm on it, boss. You got the number for me?"

Diesel pulled out his cell and said, "I'll text it to you. Hang on."

Flint settled into a chair on the opposite side of the desk, cell phone at the ready. After a few more seconds he said, "Got it," and began tapping on his phone.

While Flint's offer to make the call for him was appreciated, Diesel had been thinking more along the lines of he'd go somewhere else to call so Diesel could get his other work done. As tempted as he was show Flint the door, his curiosity overruled that instinct, and he quietly watched as Flint drummed his fingers on his desktop waiting for someone to pick up his call.

Flint stopped drumming. "Is this Topper?" He made eye contact with Diesel and nodded. "Flint from the Heathens. I'm returning your call to our President, Diesel. He's tied up but asked if I'd call you back on his behalf." More silence.

Diesel watched as Flint's features rearranged from slightly bored to slightly interested to brow furrowed and finally to full on shock.

"Why do you say that?" Flint asked. "Really. I'd say that's a *very* interesting proposition. Yes, I am speaking on behalf of our President and the club. What timeframe?" Flint reached across Diesel's desk and grabbed a sheet of paper and a pen and began writing. "Did you say Monday?" His wild-eyed gaze shot up to meet Diesel's.

What the hell were they talking about? Diesel wished he'd returned the call instead of delegating it to Flint, but nevertheless, witnessing it live was almost as good. Too bad Flint's handwriting sucked balls because he couldn't make out a single letter of what he'd written down so far.

"No, man, I appreciate the heads-up. I'll pass this on to Diesel. I'm sure he'll get back to you soon. I think we can find a nice opportunity in the situation to suit us both. Take it easy, man." Flint disconnected the call and tossed the pen on top of the desk. He leaned back in the chair, arms crossed at his chest.

Diesel shook his head at Flint's dramatic pause and posturing. "Cut the theatrics, Flint, and tell me what he said."

"He said they were providing scrubbed titles to the Gargoyles and the Titans, only the Titans got wind of it and told them to drop the Gargoyles or they'd stop playing in Peoria, so to speak." Flint paused and chuckled.

Diesel was losing his patience. He circled his hand in front of Flint's face. "And?"

"And first they told them to fuck off, then—here's where it gets good—Rotten from the Titans told him that they won't have much of a choice after the Titans wipe out the Gargoyles for torching their clubhouse, told 'em the Rebels could pick another club in the Detroit area—any club except the Gargoyles ... for now. That 'for now' part ain't so nice, of course." Flint smirked, clearly amused by the news.

Diesel's brain whirred at the possibilities in front of him "So, the Titans know the Gargoyles were behind the bomb?"

"Yep."

"And they're planning to retaliate."

"That's how it sounded."

Conflicting emotions waged a war for headspace in Diesel's thoughts. He didn't give a shit about Spider and the rest of the Gargoyles, was happy they were going to be busted for the bombing and the drugs. On the other hand, Thorn's being back with Spider put her in the crosshairs, too. "And the Rebels are taking them seriously enough to reach out to us to replace their arrangement with the Gargoyles?"

Flint tapped his nose and said, "Got it in one. Knew there was a reason we voted for you to be President."

Diesel grabbed his pen and tapped it on his desk, his thoughts churning through the implications of what Flint had relayed. He hadn't heard of any retaliation events. There was no word out on the street, not on the Detroit streets at least. Might the Rebels be fishing for something else? Some other reason to contact the Heathens with the story about their biggest rival gang no more than a worm on a hook?

"There's something odd about this." His gaze remained on the pen he rhythmically tapped against his desk.

"You can call him back yourself, you know," Flint volunteered.

That snapped his focus and brought his head up quickly, his gaze locked with Flint's. "I have a really bad feeling about this."

"Sure sounds like a win-win to me, boss. What's the problem? The Gargoyles get taken out and we get a faster route to market."

Diesel reached for his phone. "I'm gonna call Rotten first, see what he'll tell me about the Gargoyles and the Rebels."

Flint leaned forward to rest his elbows on Diesel's desk. "You sure you want to mess with a Chicago MC? Those guys shoot first and ask questions later."

Unfazed by the warning from his second in command, Diesel dialed Rotten's number. The man lived up to his name and Diesel would never want to get on his bad side, but there was more going on between the Gargoyles and the Titans.

"Diesel!" a man's voice said after the first ring.

Diesel pointed to Flint and then the door. His

second in command rolled his eyes but left the office, closing the door silently behind him.

"How'd you know it was me?" Diesel asked.

"Your caller ID said T. Reese. I may not know what the T stands for, but I know T. Reese is the president of the Detroit Heathens, AKA the famous Diesel. What can I do for you?"

"I'm doing some rumor control or confirmation about—"

"Damn that's some fast traveling news, but I can neither confirm nor deny anything you might have heard," Rotten said, laughing.

Laughing? Rotten was laughing? Diesel had only met Rotten maybe half a dozen times, but in every encounter the man was as dour and threatening as they came. Diesel had never been afraid to talk to him, even to disagree with him. He felt a certain kinship to Rotten, had a strong sense that their underlying philosophies were pretty similar. Everyone knew Rotten had grown up on the streets, taking care of a little sister on his own and dodging Child Protective Services at every corner. Diesel wished he'd been brave and tough enough at sixteen to do the same. Rotten definitely knew how to take care of his own. His sister, Violet, had gone to college, and then onto med school, and Rotten couldn't be prouder. That would have to be Diesel's angle.

"You obviously know what I'm talking about," Diesel said. "Listen though, I wouldn't normally give a shit about what goes down with the Heathens' number one rival, but I try to look out for one of Spider's gang, someone I grew up with."

Rotten grunted. "Not sure why that would be my problem."

"Maybe not your problem but I figured since you watched out for your sister all those years and probably still do—Violet, right? Isn't she a nurse over at Peabody General? Over in Gargoyle territory?"

"She's a resident, almost a doctor—but she ain't got nothing to do with this!" The big man's voice boomed with concern intermixed with the anger. As expected, Rotten would never stand for anyone messing with his family.

"I know. My point has nothing to do with your sister, specifically. I only meant, you'd do anything to protect her, right? Even with her in the heart of Gargoyle territory, you'd do whatever you needed to do to protect your sister, am I right?"

"What's your point, Diesel?"

"My point is if you and your guys are going to pay a house call to the Gargoyles—and believe me, I got no beef with that. You guys gotta have good reason to do whatever you're planning—I'm asking for a chance to get my friend out of the way before anything goes down. That's all. A word of warning."

The line went silent for a second, a good sign. "Who's your friend? How do I know you won't tip off the Gargoyles by saving this friend?"

It was Diesel's turn to laugh. "My friend isn't a Gargoyle's officer or VIP. I believe in street justice. I also believe the enemy of my enemy is my friend."

Rotten sighed. "We friends now?" He chuckled softly.

"Situationally speaking." The clock on Diesel's wall read a quarter past seven. The sun would be setting soon, and sundown usually ushered in scores being settled in secluded allies, brokered deals in pool halls and bowling allies before the regulars claimed them for their tournaments and leagues. He had a lot of business to take care of in the upcoming hours and needed to reach some sort of accord with Rotten soon.

"Well … my friend … I don't think you have anything to worry about."

Diesel's brow furrowed. "How so?"

"You see, I'm like a surgeon. I see a cancer and I go in and cut out only the diseased tissue, leave the rest of the body alone. I got no quarrel with the Gargoyles as a club, other than a mutual supplier that was getting its priorities backwards. But that's old news."

The supplier would be the Rebels, of course. "I see." He wanted to mention the bombing but he couldn't be sure that's what Rotten was talking about, and he knew to play his own cards equally close to the vest.

"My issue is with Spider and Spider only, so your friend shouldn't be in any danger."

Diesel closed his eyes and exhaled slowly as relief flooded his body, relaxing his muscles. The Titans' revenge was targeted

"Only Spider and his old lady have anything to worry about."

Diesel stiffened in his chair, the hairs on his arms standing on end. "Spider's old lady? Why would you target her?"

"Before he died, my father taught me that when you want to take down your opponent and keep him down long enough time to ponder how he got there, you don't break a single leg. You gotta break both. One break slows your enemy down. Two breaks take him down and keep him down, give him time to think about things, reconsider."

Diesel's heart raced and pounded in his ears. If he exposed Thorn as the "friend" he was watching out for he'd only be upping her value as an Achilles heel in case Rotten had a larger agenda than a little revenge against the Gargoyles. How then could he get more details about the planned hit on Spider and by extension, Thorn?

119

Very carefully.

"Not knocking your skills as a surgeon, Rotten, but I can't risk my friend being in the wrong place at the wrong time. I'm going to need more than that."

"Why should I change any of my plans on the off chance your friend is having a three-way with Spider and his old lady at an inconvenient time? Sorry, my friend, but we'll both have to leave that up to chance and hope for the best."

The line went dead.

Chapter Thirteen

Thorn nudged the shower's temperature control lever further to the left for the third time. The hot water heater was giving up the last of the warm water begrudgingly. She didn't want to get out, didn't want to have sex with Spider, but she also didn't want to deny him. Sex on demand had always been an unspoken agreement between Thorn and Spider. It ran both ways, but Thorn rarely felt the need to initiate because Spider's sex drive was practically insatiable. She'd never minded before. She minded now. Things had changed. She had changed, but so had Spider.

The drugs had changed him. Spider doing or dealing drugs was insurmountable in Thorn's book, and Spider knew it or had every reason to know it. As often as they'd discussed her feelings on the subject, Thorn felt the sting of his dealing as the ultimate "fuck you". He didn't care what she thought, didn't care that he'd broken her number one taboo. He expected her to fall back into line because keeping her around, even in a loveless relationship, was more important to his ego and power hold on the Gargoyles than her or even his own emotional needs.

Hell, who was she kidding? Spider didn't love her. She wondered if he ever had. She was more of a figurehead than a girlfriend or old lady. The other brutal truth was *she* had changed. Being with Trey again, even with his new identity as Diesel, had awakened something in her she thought had died. It hadn't. Like Sleeping Beauty, she'd been kissed into consciousness, only there was no prince around to claim her.

The water cooled, and Thorn was forced to finally shut off the shower. Her waterlogged skin had wrinkled and turned an unhealthy milky shade. The large Turkish towel she wrapped around her body was the warm embrace she craved but knew she wouldn't get from Spider. She wrapped a second towel around her hair and began to apply lotion to her skin, anything to stall their reunion. Next, she combed her hair, removing all the tangles from her curls. She wouldn't blow out her tresses into sleek strands even if that was how Spider preferred it, even if it would give her another twenty minutes before going to his bed.

Finally, she squared her shoulders and whispered to her reflection, "Tonight you appease him. Tomorrow you start taming him all over again."

Her reflection rolled its eyes and whispered back, "Spider won't be tamed, and there is no point in pining for another. There never was. Best you get both of those facts through your thick skull, Thorn." She made a fist and knocked her knuckles against her forehead.

Hand on the bathroom doorknob, Thorn paused for a second to draw in and slowly release a calming breath. She could do this. Spider was her life, her future. Diesel was her past, and there was a sobering truth to the saying "you can't go back". She needed to get him out of her head, out of her heart. They had no future.

The knob turned and she opened the door, but to her surprise, the bed and room were empty. "Spider?"

No one answered. There was no sound other than her own breathing and the beating of her nervous heart.

Spider's clothes lay in unruly heaps on the floor by the bed. Did that mean he was naked in another room in the condo? Or had he changed clothes and left? Was it likely that karma had taken pity on her? Thorn slipped back into the bathroom and pulled on her thick terrycloth robe and slippers. Spider might traipse around nude in the condo, but she didn't. Too many open windows visible to the neighbors whose silent judgments of her appearance she didn't want to chance.

She padded silently down the hallway. If Spider was still in the condo, he was being quieter than usual. The guest bathroom and bedrooms were empty. The only other room left on the second level was a game room/loft that overlooked the main floor. Spider wasn't there either. Kitchen, perhaps? Getting a drink or a snack? She had taken her sweet time in the shower, though amazingly he hadn't come pounding on the door telling her to hurry up.

Slowly, Thorn headed down the stairs. She wanted to see him before he saw her, if only to have a chance to gauge his state of mind and adjusting hers to match or confront.

He wasn't in the kitchen, but a crash coming from the laundry room caught her attention. She glided down the remaining steps, taking care to keep as quiet as possible. Another series of impacts, like flesh against flesh, followed by male groans. Thorn puzzled over the strange sounds. *If he's having sex with some Bunny in our house, I will fucking kill him and maim her!*

A strange man's voice drifted to her ears. Her disgust at the idea that he might be banging some girl in their home while she was there dissolved. A tinge of shame took its place that she'd been so quick to jump to a nasty conclusion. She moved closer until she could make out the words being said.

"Where is she?" the man asked.

"I told you. She's out shopping." Spider's voice.

Who was the man with Spider? Who were they talking about? Who was out shopping? Her? One of his fucking Bunnies? Spider knew she was in the shower, so why would he lie about it? There were no grudges against her, no vendettas. She was an extension of Spider … but that also made her a weapon to use against him.

Oh shit! This is bad, real bad.

"Guess we need to take a look around then. Hope we don't accidentally break stuff," the other man said. A loud crash followed.

"Fuck y—*oof*!" What sounded like a punch to the gut cut him off. Spider coughed and then wheezed, "Told you. She's … not … here."

Spider was hurt, and they were coming after her next! Were the men going to kill them both? Mess them up badly? Rape her in front of Spider and then kill them? She didn't need to use her imagination to know that type of shit went down in other places. Detroit wasn't exempt from brutal turf warfare.

What could she do? Fear tangled her thoughts. Her breaths were rapid and shallow. Her heart battered her chest wall, urging her to fight or flight. It was smarter than she was. *Focus, Thorn!* She needed a weapon. She needed to call someone from the club to send help fast! Problem was her cell was in her purse and her purse was by the front door. The battery had to be low. She'd meant to put it on the charger but had forgotten.

Shit! Where was Spider's cell? Back in the bedroom with his clothes? Probably if he was naked. If he'd dressed in different clothes, he might have it in his pocket. They had no land line. Their computer was in the living room, too close to the laundry room. No chance using it to send out an SOS. She hoped Spider's gun was under the mattress.

Time was critical. She made her decision and retraced her steps back to the bedroom, locking the door behind her. She plunged her hand beneath the mattress sweeping back and forth. Gone. The gun was gone. Thorn cursed under her breath. Had he taken it with him when he confronted those thugs? Did they have it now?

Too late to worry about that. She had to move on to option two. Call for help and hope it arrived in time.

Finding Spider's cast-off clothing, she patted the pockets of his shirt but found nothing. His pants were more promising. In the hip pocket was his wallet. She found his cell phone in the front pocket. If he had changed clothes, he'd been interrupted before he could transfer his wallet and cell over.

Thorn tapped the phone's screen only to find it was locked. She had no idea what four-digit code Spider had set to unlock the screen. 1-2-3-4 didn't work, and neither did 9-9-9-9. *Crap, crap, crap! What now?* Her heart pounded harder and more insistently with every second that ticked by. A coil of panic was rapidly unfurling in her gut. She couldn't allow it to overtake her, to paralyze her into inaction. Eyes closed, she forced herself to draw in a deep breath that she held then slowly released. *Think, Thorn, think!*

911. She'd have to call 911. Even locked phones allowed emergency calls out. A few taps later the line rang and a dispatcher answered, "911, what is your emergency?"

Keeping her voice soft, Thorn said, "Intruder ... there's an intruder in my home. I think ... I think he's attacking my boyfriend. Please hurry! I'm at 777 Northeast Fairmont St., Unit 3B. It's a four-plex condo building. Hurry! Please!"

"All right, ma'am. Stay on the line with me, okay? Help is on the way. Do you know how many intruders there are? Male or female?"

Thorn's breath continued to come in shallow pants. She needed to do something, not shoot the breeze with the operator. Spider might be hurt or worse! "I—I can't tell. I think I heard two men, but I didn't see them. My boyfriend might be hurt. We have to get help here fast! They're looking for me now!"

"Where are they, and where are you?" the 911

operator asked.

"Upstairs. In the bedroom. I locked the door. My boyfriend is downstairs, in the laundry room. I could hear them but couldn't see them. They didn't see me. He told them I wasn't here, but they don't believe him. They'll be looking for me soon." Thorn paused, the phone pulled away from her ear as she listened for any signs the man or men were coming upstairs for her.

"Ma'am? Ma'am? Are you still there? Do they know you're in the house?"

"I don't know. My boyfriend does. The guy keeps asking him where 'she' is. I assume he means me."

Men's voices were growing louder outside her bedroom door. "Oh God! They're coming upstairs. Please, hurry! I gotta hide, gotta get out of here."

"I understand. Help is on the way. Is there a closet you can hide in or a bathroom with a lock? Anything to put more barriers between you and these men?"

"A-a bathroom. I could go—"

A loud crash interrupted her. The bedroom door flew open, and two men wearing ski masks stepped inside. They spotted her instantly and moved toward her.

Thorn screamed, "Get out! I'm on the phone with the cops. They're on their way!"

The first man to enter the room laughed, and after a glance at his companion said, "Told you that punk was lying. She was up here the whole time, freshly fucked."

Though much closer, Thorn still didn't recognize their voices. The first man was tall and lanky like a basketball player, several inches taller than six feet. His companion was much shorter—maybe five foot ten—but extremely buff like a weightlifter. They both wore dark jeans and black t-shirts. Their ski masks were also black.

The two men stopped advancing on her when

they reached the foot of the bed. The bulky one said, "Hang up. Now." Hoops nodded and then lunged toward, batting the phone from her hand where it went skittering across the floor. Too shocked to scream, Thorn jumped away before Hoops could grab her. From her vantage point, she noticed the edge of a baseball bat sticking out from the space between her nightstand and the wall. Once upon a time Spider had cared enough to stash the crude weapon on her side of the bed. She'd laughed at the gesture then. Now, she prayed she could grab it and use it before they grabbed her.

"Get away from me," Thorn snarled. She shifted from foot to foot, hoping to inch her way close enough to grab the bat. And then what? They didn't appear to have guns or knives. Maybe she had a fighting chance if she could get the bat.

"Sorry, chickie, but Doctor's orders are to make an example of you and Spider." The Bulk flexed his arms making his biceps pop. "And I gotta say taking care of you will be a hell of lot more fun than taking care of your old man was."

Thorn swallowed. Where was Spider? Had they beaten him so badly he couldn't move? Was he tied up? Was he even alive? What would they do to her? Rape her? Beat her? Kill her? And why? Who were they? Somebody Spider had crossed? Surely not any of the Heathens. She needed that bat, and she needed it now! Thorn dropped low and lunged for the bat. Her fingers found the grip and tugged it out of its hiding place. "Back the fuck off, motherfuckers!" She raised the bat into position, ready to strike any man who made a move.

Hoops and Bulk paused as if assessing her threat level. "I wouldn't piss us off if I were you. You'll only make it worse for you and Spider," Bulk said, beginning to move closer.

Thorn swung the bat forcing Bulk to reverse course. "I said get out!"

Hoops took a couple of steps to the side, cutting off more of her escape route. If they closed in on her, she might be able to take out one but not both. Bulk cocked his head to the side as if giving silent instructions to Hoops. Hoops took a step closer to her.

Thorn swung in a wide arc around her space, but before she could bring her arms back in close to her body, Hoops shot forward and seized the end of the bat. He shoved against it so hard Thorn lost her balance and fell against the wall, loosening Hoops's hold on the end. Bulk charged in from the other side, but Thorn was faster. The bat connected with a sickening thwack against one of his knees. Howling in pain, Bulk fell to the floor holding his right leg. The distraction, however, gave Hoops a second opportunity to attack. He did by kicking the bat out of her hands. He reached for her arm and jerked her to her feet. With his free hand, Hoops punched Thorn in the side of her head.

Woozy from the blow, Thorn struggled to stay on her feet. Everything spun, and she lost all sense of up versus down. Sounds were muffled as if passing through giant wads of cotton in her ears. She felt a momentary sense of weightlessness before coming to rest on the bed, defenseless.

"I'm not fucking playing around anymore with you, bitch!" Hoops spat out, his tone full of menace before giving Thorn a vicious slap across the face. "So now, you fucking cunt, it's time to get down to business. You guys started something with the Titans you're going to regret."

"The Titans," Thorn whispered. Her vision was still unfocused and blurry. Cold metal pressed against her throat making it hard to breathe. A heavy weight pushed her into the mattress, and then everything went black.

Chapter Fourteen

"Are you nuts? You can't stroll up to Spider's place and knock on the door like you're paying a social call." Flint's hand gestures had become more and more frantic as he tried but failed to talk Diesel out of his suicide mission.

"It's too late to come up with any other idea. Something's going down—now—I feel it. No matter what our differences are with the Gargoyles, the last thing we want is some gang from Chicago trying to muscle into Detroit by using a vendetta as leverage." Diesel slipped his pistol in his concealed carry harness, zipped his jacket. He'd already stashed a knife in the side of his boot. He was done arguing with Flint and was ready to go, with or without his lieutenant.

"You can't say you don't think Spider deserves whatever the Titans might dish out. He bombed their clubhouse, Diesel. Nobody lets that sort of shit go unpunished. You wouldn't, would you?" Flint moved between Diesel and the door, the fingers of his hand pressing against Diesel's chest. "Would you?"

"Flint." Diesel drew in a deep breath through his nose, held it for a count of three, then exhaled. "Look. We don't know why Spider did what he did. Also, you weren't on the call with Rotten. I've been thinking it over—what Rotten said, what the Rebels said. Something isn't adding up. And no one's ever figured out why Spider decided to bomb the Titans. What the hell was that about anyway? Spider's a fucktard, but he's not stupid."

Flint dropped his hand to his side. "Fine. All right. But let me and Python and a couple of other guys come with."

"No. Too many and we're taking too big a chance of being seen as a threat. You and Python can give me ten minutes' lead, then hold back unless you see there's trouble." Diesel shouldered past Flint, through the open doorway and toward the garage where his bike was parked.

****

Diesel ran through a million different scenarios of what he might find when he reached Spider's place from the two of them watching television oblivious to the danger they're in to a gruesome bloodbath. He pushed the latter scene from his mind. Losing Cathy wasn't an option.

He pulled to the curb of Spider's condo and surveyed the dark windows. From the outside it appeared no one was home. Doubt swirled in his head. Maybe they were at the Gargoyles' clubhouse celebrating Thorn's return. His gaze steadied on an upstairs window where he could've sworn he saw a shadow. Diesel cut his engine and left his helmet on his seat before striding to the front door. He listened for a moment. An eerie silence blanketed the dark entryway. Wrapping his palm around the doorknob he slowly twisted until he heard a click and the door cracked open. Before stepping inside, he pulled the knife from his boot, slid it into the sleeve of his jacket and snapped the cuff securing it inside, then took his pistol from the harness inside his jacket.

From where he stood it appeared the entire first floor was dark except for a soft glow from what was probably the kitchen. He crept toward the light as his eyesight adjusted to the darkness. A muffled sound like something heavy dragging on the floor came from the kitchen followed by a grunt. Diesel backed against the wall and slowly peeked into the room. A series of thick deep red lines decorated the white tiled floor. His gaze followed the tracks to a set of large bare feet covered in blood. Diesel stepped closer. His eyes trailed up the naked, crumpled, and bloodied body on the floor.

"Jesus. Spider?" He stepped over the form and crouched next to Spider's face.

Spider's bruised and swollen eyes fluttered open. His dark pupils looked right through him. "Thorn," he mouthed.

"Where is she?"

Spider groaned as he tried to move his arm.

"Just tell me where she is?"

"Upstairs. I tried … I tried to tell them she wasn't here. I tried…"

"Fuck." It was his worst nightmare. Knowing what they did to Spider stabbed at his chest, wondering what they did to Cathy. Rotten's words rang through his head: *You don't break a single leg. You gotta break both.*

Diesel raced to the staircase and taking the carpeted stairs two at a time, the cool steel of his pistol drawn to his chest. He froze at the top of the stairs. Two arguing male voices carried down the hallway.

"Let's get outta here. She said she called the cops."

The deeper voice answered, "You know what you have to do. Boss's orders. He wants to send a message to Spider. He fucks with us and we fuck his old lady. You got to if you want to be fully patched."

Diesel moved closer until he had a view into the bedroom. His gaze landed on Cathy lying on the bed, her white robe open, exposing her breasts. His first impulse was to blow both of their brains out, but he also knew it would set off a bigger war between the clubs. His gaze ticked back to Cathy, and he watched the rise and fall of her chest. Her breath was even. As long as he didn't let them touch her she'd be okay. The men continued their squabble.

"Rape an unconscious girl? I can't. Can't we *say*

we did it? She won't know the difference anyway," the taller one said. He sounded like a kid even though he was tall enough to be an NBA point guard.

The shorter one who looked like a steroid junkie spat back. "Jesus Christ, you're a pussy. You don't have what it takes to be a Titan. Hold the gun and watch a man get the job done."

It was Diesel's cue to strike. "I'll give you one chance to drop the gun and get the fuck away from her."

The two men looked up at the same time seemingly in shock to see Diesel standing in the doorway. Their ski masks hid their expressions, but even through the covering, Diesel could tell the tall, young one was scared shitless. His hands shook as he tried to point the gun in Diesel's direction. Diesel took a step into the room. "Drop the gun or you bought your friend a bullet between the eyes. Your boss won't like losing one of his members."

The gun jumped in the tall guy's grasp.

"Don't listen to him, he won't shoot us."

"No? That's my girl there. You fucking better believe I'll shoot you."

"Your girl? This is Spider's old lady."

"Not anymore." That was the last time anyone would refer to Cathy like that.

"Trey?" Cathy's head turned slowly toward him.

"I'm here." He couldn't help moving his focus to her for a moment, reassuring her with a smile, which turned out to be a big fucking mistake. The young buck let off a shot that whizzed by his temple, setting Diesel off balance right before the mass of muscle rammed him to the floor knocking the gun from his grasp. Even though Diesel had a number of inches over the guy, his attacker had twice the muscle mass. Diesel's attempt to throw a few punches at the guy's jaw and temple seemed to do more harm to Diesel's already raw knuckles. Diesel doubled over from a full force blow to his kidney, giving him the opportunity to access the weapon he'd hidden in his sleeve.

A flash of silver reflected in the asshole's eye before the blade sank into his abdomen right below his ribcage. He screamed out in pain. "You fucking stabbed me!"

Diesel yanked the knife from his side and held it to the man's face as blood dripped over his fingers. "Want another? I saved your lung that time, but that usually happens only once."

The guy clutched the wound site as a dark circle grew in size over his shirt. He took a few unsteady steps backward. "You're a crazy motherfucker," he yelled before stumbling down the hall and from the sound of it, tumbled down the stairs.

His partner's hand fell to his side, his mouth wide open in shock. Sirens blared in the distance. "Drop the gun, Stretch, and I'll tell the cops you didn't follow that fucker's orders."

The gun dropped with a thud, and he pulled the mask off and rubbed his palm over his face. "I don't want to hurt anyone. I don't know what I'm doing here."

Diesel nodded. He saw his younger self in the kid. "You don't want this life," Diesel said before moving to Cathy's side. He carefully closed her robe, covering her exposed flesh. Her head moved from side to side and her eyes fluttered as she tried to say something. "Shhh. Don't try to talk, Cath. You're safe now."

"Is she gonna be okay?"

Diesel inspected her neck. An angry red line glowed against her light mocha skin. As sickening as it looked, Diesel knew she'd heal. "Yes. Spider's in worse shape. You better hope he lives or you can kiss your chance of a normal life good-bye. And your piece of shit buddy will be okay too as long as he doesn't lose too much blood. I purposely stabbed him where there are no internal organs." It was another survival tip he'd learned on the streets. Maiming someone in self-defense looked better in the courts than murder.

Police lights flashed from outside throwing red and blue shadows on the walls. "I'll go check on him."

"Hey," Diesel called and the man stopped. "What's your name?"

"They call me T-Bone," he said quietly without turning around.

"Your real name."

"My name's Mark."

"Do yourself a favor, Mark. If you get out of this thing, get away from the MC. Far away. Make your mother proud and do something good with your second chance." For all Diesel knew Mark was motherless like himself, but pulling the mom card was worth a shot.

Mark hung his head and shuffled down the hall as a commotion sounded from the first floor.

Diesel stroked Cathy's cheek, focusing on her and only vaguely aware of the chaos going on below.

"Put your hands up!"

"Don't shoot. Please. I'm not armed," Mark pleaded. "There are two guys down here who are hurt bad and a lady upstairs."

Diesel pulled Thorn into his arms. "Can you hear me?" He lightly pressed two fingers to her neck. A rapid but strong pulse responded to his touch.

She moaned, her hand trailed up her robe and rested on his arm. "Trey?"

"It's me, baby. Everything's going to be okay. You're safe." He repeated the words until her eyes blinked open.

"What happened? Two men. They broke in." Her eyes darted across the room. "Are they—"

"They're not going to hurt you or anyone else. Cops are downstairs now."

"Spider?"

"He's in bad shape, but I hear an ambulance coming." He was glad Cathy didn't see Spider's broken and blood-soaked body. Diesel had doubts he'd survive his injuries.

He cradled her as footsteps bound up the stairs and stomped down the hall. Within seconds the room was filled with uniformed officers, detectives, and emergency responders shouting questions. He was asked to stand to be patted down for weapons. "You satisfied now? I'm not the enemy here."

"Just doing our jobs," the detective said and arched his brow.

Diesel knew the guy as Shadow. He was the Heathens' informant and inside guy at the DPD, whom Diesel paid generously for his services. To everyone else he was Detective Jack McGuinness. He wondered for a split second how much Shadow knew about the undercover operation targeting the Gargoyles. Maybe ol' Shadow was passing intel on to the Gargoyles, too. He couldn't worry about that now though. Cathy was hurt. Diesel offered a slight nod before jockeying around EMTs and detectives who were examining and questioning Cathy.

She shook her head. "I don't remember anything after they broke into the room." Her brows knitted together.

"Look, she's in shock. How about you give her a break?"

The other detective nodded and shifted her attention to Diesel. "We can get her statement at the hospital. Tell me what you know."

Diesel gave the detective a detailed account of what happened when he found Cathy, wrapping it up as the EMT finished examining Cathy. "How is she?" Diesel asked.

"She sustained blunt force trauma to her head. I suspect a concussion. She'll need to be observed overnight."

Flint rushed into the bedroom. "Deez. You okay? They wouldn't let us in. All I saw was Spider and another guy brought out on stretchers."

"How's Spider?" Diesel asked.

"I dunno. He looked real banged up, but he's still on this side of the daisies so that's good news for him at least."

Diesel lifted Cathy and helped her onto the stretcher. "I'll be with you every step of the way," he whispered in her ear and before EMTS carried her down the stairs.

Police tape littered the entire first floor, blocking off bloodied trails and footprints. Spotting Mark in the back of a DPD cruiser as he followed the stretcher outside, Diesel nodded toward McGuinness as he passed. "The kid was a pawn in this."

"I figured. We'll scare him 'til he craps his pants and let him go."

"Good man," Diesel said and climbed into the back of the ambulance.

He asked about Spider's condition on the way to the hospital. Several broken bones and probable internal injuries were all their EMT knew. Cathy sipped some water in the ambulance and the EMT said her vitals looked good.

Rotten's man did exactly what he was supposed to do: sent a message without collateral damage. Thank

God Diesel got there before anything else happened.

Chapter Fifteen

Diesel hated hospitals. They reminded him of his foster homes: cold, impersonal, and transient. A place no one wanted to be but had little choice in the matter. He followed Cathy's stretcher as its wheels squealed along the white linoleum floor. Double doors marked with big red "ER" letters banged open, and they brought her gurney to a halt in one of the curtained cubbyholes. Diesel scanned the unit. This wouldn't do. Too open. Too vulnerable. He had no idea what Rotten's next move would be, but he sure as shit wasn't about to let Cathy sit like a carnival plastic duck floating in a barrel of water waiting to be picked off for a prize. He should've insisted on taking her back to his place.

"Hey!" he called to the nearest scrub-wearing person with a stethoscope around the neck.

The woman looked up from a folder she was reading. "How may I help you?" She was younger than he originally assumed and he immediately thought she wouldn't be able to do anything for him, but it was worth a try.

"I need my friend moved to a private room with a door and security. I don't care what it costs."

"Private rooms are for admitted patients. Your friend has to be assessed first before we decide where she'll go."

"Look, Nurse…" Diesel peered at her name tag. "Sanchez. This is important."

"First, it's Dr. Sanchez. I'm a third year ER resident. Second, all of our patients are important. Third, there's a hospital protocol. Patients are assessed and stabilized in the ER, so if I were you, I'd claim one of those chairs over there—they are the least uncomfortable—and wait your turn. It's a busy night.

Must be a full moon. Excuse me," Dr. Sanchez said, waving a dismissive hand and turning her attention back to her folder as she disappeared through a curtain into another cubby.

He dragged one of the chairs she pointed out through the curtain of Cathy's unit. "Can I get you something? Water? A beer?" he asked settling the chair next to her bed.

Cathy offered a weak chuckle and palmed her forehead. "It hurts to laugh."

"You scared the shit out of me, you know?" He rested his arm on the edge of the bed and stroked the top of her hand with this thumb.

"I don't know when you got there, but you saved me, didn't you? Thank God you were there. Spider. He— he told them I wasn't home. He tried…" Her voice trailed off.

"He tried to protect you. I know. He told me." He remembered the pain in Spider's voice.

"He's not all that bad."

Diesel shook his head once. "No. He's not all that bad," Diesel said studying her face. "Do you love him, Cath? Because if you do, it's okay. I'll stay here with you and protect you until he's recovered. If you want to go back to him, I'll hate it, but I'll deal." He almost choked on his words, but he had to know what was going on in her head. Diesel held his breath as he waited for her answer.

"I never loved Spider. Not like that. And I'm pretty sure he never loved me that way either. We were thrown together. He felt an obligation to take care of me. I felt an obligation to be with him. Then the club happened, and all of a sudden he was president and I was his old lady, and there was no going back. Then with all this ugliness—the drugs, the bombs, the wars with rival clubs—I don't know who he is anymore. I don't think he does either." She tilted her head. "As for you, you never listen to me, do you?"

Relief flooded through him, and he chuckled. "What do you mean?"

Her fingers curled around his and she lifted his hand, examining the dried blood covering his knuckles. "I told you to stop punching things."

He shrugged. "Seems to be an occupational hazard of protecting you."

She smiled. "Try punching some sense into your hard head. Wasn't it obvious how I felt about you when I was at your house?"

"You mean when you cursed me out and risked your life trying to escape? I really felt the love, Cath," he teased.

"You know what I mean. In the kitchen? Our kiss. God, I couldn't stop thinking about it. I can't stop thinking about it."

His heart sang, and suddenly he felt like they were teenagers again, filled with hope and passion. "Remember when I told you I left you *because* I loved you?"

Cathy nodded but her mouth tightened at the edges like she was steeling herself for bad news. That was on him, but he would grab this second chance and fix it once and for all.

"That wasn't completely true." Her gaze lowered, and he hooked his index finger under her chin. "Hey," he said softly, and when her eyes flicked up, his heart almost bottomed out. "What I should've told you was I never *stopped* loving you. Not for a second." He leaned toward her, and his gaze landed on her lips. Her hand trailed to the back of his neck drawing him in, pulling his mouth to hers.

A swish of the curtain dragged him back to the present. "Excuse me." Diesel stood and turned to see the resident, Dr. Sanchez, standing next to the curtain with another woman in scrubs at her side. The doctor stepped inside and motioned her hand toward the woman saying, "This is Monica, the ER nurse on duty tonight. She'll need to get some information from Ms. Rose, and I'll need you to step out with me."

Diesel squeezed Cathy's hand. "I'll be outside, back as soon as I can."

After the Dr. Sanchez closed the curtain she said, "Can I speak to you a moment?" She tipped her head to the bank of chairs a few feet away.

Diesel nodded and slid the chair so he had a view of Cathy's unit and the door leading to the ER. "What's up?"

"I was told Ms. Rose was brought in from the same address as two other men tonight."

"That's true. It was a break and enter."

"For what? Burglary? Was anything taken?"

Diesel narrowed his eyes. "Not sure that's relevant to her medical condition."

Dr. Sanchez leaned forward and lowered her voice. "I'll level with you. I need to know if this was club-related."

"I don't know what you're talking about," Diesel said. All club business was private between clubs, even those at war with each other.

"You're full of shit. I know who you are, and I know who she is. I also know the guy in surgery right now getting his broken bones wired back together nearly killed my brother," she said with an urgent whisper.

"Your brother?" Diesel's gaze dropped to the employee badge hanging from a lanyard around her neck: Violet Sanchez. Damn it, he should've put it together. "You're Rotten's sister?"

"I hate that name, but yes, Roberto Sanchez is my brother. Is this because of him? Was he taking revenge on the Gargoyles for the bomb?"

"I don't know," Diesel lied.

"Yes, you do. It's the reason you asked for a private room and the reason you can't take your eyes away from that curtain. You're afraid for her safety because you interrupted what Rotten sent his men to do."

She was one hundred percent correct. "Look, Cathy's a good friend of mine, and I'm here to make sure she's okay."

"You have a habit of kissing other club presidents' old ladies?"

Damn, Rotten's sister knew all the clubs' business. Diesel rubbed his face. "It's not what it seems. It's complicated."

"It always is. What you do is your business, but my brother is mine. If he was responsible for this I need to know."

"Why?"

"Because I took an oath to heal and do no harm."

"That's you, not your brother."

"I became a doctor to help people, not to help people Roberto beats to a pulp or sends his men to mess up for the sole reason of who they are with. I can't and won't allow him to do that."

"I don't agree with Rotten's ways either, especially dragging Cathy into it, but if Spider was the one responsible for the Titan bombing, I get why Rotten wanted revenge. He has a responsibility to protect his club, just like I have a responsibility to protect mine. The guy they sent to do the job—who is he?"

She tilted her head. "You mean the guy you stabbed? You almost pierced his lung."

"It was far enough away to think I did but not close enough to do any real damage."

"You grew up in the streets."

"Damn right," Diesel said proudly.

"His name is Griller. He's one of the Titan's officers. He's a patient here. I'm not going to tell you where because I don't want any trouble."

"He hurt my girl and was about to … he had his filthy hands on her. Thank God I got there when I did and stopped him or he'd be needing a lot more than a couple stitches and an IV of antibiotics."

Violet pinched the bridge of her nose with her thumb and index finger. "Look, I gave you information. Do me a solid and don't throw down any shit here. Save it for another day and definitely another place."

"Will do, doctor." Diesel gave her a mock salute.

"So, Spider not only had his face bashed in, several other broken bones, plus some life-threatening internal injuries, but to top it off he also lost his old lady?"

"It's a shitty day to be Spider. Can't say I feel bad for the guy though. He was asking for it."

She blew out a tired breath. "I'm assigned to his recovery. Trauma's my specialty."

"You're assigned to help the guy who tried to bomb your brother? That'll put the Hippocratic Oath to the test, eh?"

She chuckled and stood. "Yeah. Now let's go see how she's doing. I'd like to get her *and you* out of here as soon as possible."

Chapter Sixteen

Diesel turned on the ignition and leaned his head against the headrest, his face toward Cathy. She met his gaze from the passenger seat. "What? I look like hell, don't I?" She flipped the visor down and peered into the mirror, smoothing the pad of her index finger over the bruise darkening her cheek.

"You look beautiful." He tucked a wayward curl behind her ear and leaned over, brushing his lips across hers. He couldn't wait to get her alone. They'd barely had a minute of privacy during the day and a half in the hospital filled with tests and questions. Cathy was finally released that afternoon with instructions to rest and recover, which Diesel vowed to make his sole focus.

While neither one of them saw Spider, Dr. Sanchez updated them that he'd pulled through surgery but would be confined to a hospital bed for a few weeks while his vitals stabilized and his broken bones were immobilized.

"Ready to go home?" he asked.

Cathy's eyes widened. "I—I can't go back to the condo. There's blood everywhere. I can't go back there."

"That's not exactly the home I had in mind. I was talking about my house. *Our* home. Yours and mine ... and Dammit, of course."

"You want me to move in with you?"

"It's what I want if you do, too. It'll be you and me against the world again. Side by side. That's my only condition."

"I like the sound of that." Her eyes sparkled, and it was the first real smile he'd seen on her lips since all those years ago. He cupped her cheek and swiped his thumb along her chin.

"I want you as an equal. I don't want you to just

be my old lady. You're so much more than that. There's so much more you can do."

"I always wanted to help kids out there who are like us. Older kids in the system who feel like no one wants them. I tried to explain it to Spider, but he just didn't get it."

Diesel nodded. It was something he'd thought about doing too. "I get it."

She nodded. "I know you do. Maybe the Heathens can start a foundation, create a place where kids can go to feel safe. It would show goodwill to the city and put a positive spin on MC clubs like the Heathens."

"You're brilliant." He laced his fingers with hers and squeezed her hand.

"No one's ever told me that before."

Diesel didn't want to take his eyes off her, but he also couldn't wait to get her home. He moved his hand to the gearshift and pushed it into reverse. He wanted to hit the gas, but he took it slow even though his heart raced at the thought of having her in his home for good and forever. He hit the brake at every turn and dodged every pothole like he was transporting something fragile. Cathy laughed at his "old man driving" and swore she needed no white glove treatment, but he didn't care. It was more a matter of what she deserved than what she needed.

Finally, Diesel steered the car into the driveway and killed the engine in front of the closed garage door.

"Wait right there, and don't open your door yet. Someone wants to see you, but I gotta make sure she doesn't get overly excited and accidentally hurt you," he said opening his car door and ignoring her renewed protests. He hurried to the front porch and unlocked the door. Dammit bound outside and immediately jumped on him, offering a sloppy kiss. He'd asked Python to care for her while he stayed with Cathy in the hospital. He knew Python wasn't Dammit's favorite person. That person used to be Diesel, but he'd been relegated to second place behind Cathy. Dammit followed Diesel to the passenger side. He held her collar as he opened the door so she wouldn't jump. Dammit's whimpers and tail thumps on Diesel's leg told him she was as excited as he was to have Cathy home.

"Good girl. Such a good girl." Cathy scratched the back of Dammit's ear. "Let's go inside, now." She swung her legs out of the car.

"Hold on. We're going to do this right." He swooped down and scooped under her knees with one arm, and put the other around her back before lifting her into her up.

"What are you doing?" she laughed.

"Carrying you into the house. Isn't that good luck or something?"

"I've been in your house, Trey, or don't you remember the whole kidnap thing?" she joked.

"You've been to my house, yes. But this is the first time you'll enter our home. Things will be different."

"You mean you don't plan to lock me in a room and tie me to a bed?"

"No locks, but I make no promises about the other one." A flame burned within him at the thought of slowly but firmly binding her wrists to his headboard and teasing her gorgeous breasts until she writhed under him.

Cathy grazed the backs of her fingers along his cheek. "Take me home."

He carefully carried her to the front door and inside. "Where to, princess?"

"Do you really need to ask?" She met his stare with fire in her eyes.

"Are you sure? I mean, they said you need to

recover."

"And I can't think of a better recovery plan," she said with a wink.

His cock shifted in his pants and his heart raced like it had the first time he'd made love to her all those years ago. But then it was eager and inexperienced breaths and whispers, trying not to get caught. Now they were both full-grown adults with wants and needs and the confidence to express them openly.

He strode to his bedroom, kicking the door closed with his foot, leaving Dammit on the other side. He set Cathy down on one side of the bed and crawled over her to the other side without breaking eye contact. He flattened his hand on her belly. Even through the material of her shirt, the heat of her flesh seared his palm. Her hands were already under his shirt at his waist, kicking his heart, and other parts of him, into higher gear. He studied her face, and a pang of guilt hit him when his gaze landed on the ugly bruise on her neck. "Are you sure? We can wait until—"

She cupped his face between her hands. "I think we've waited long enough, don't you?"

He answered with a slow kiss that grew in heat as she parted her lips and it was like starved man on Thanksgiving. He couldn't remember how long it had been since he kissed a woman like that, let alone anything else. All he'd ever wanted was Cathy, and now that she was finally his, he was going to enjoy the feast set before him. He dipped his tongue inside and it all came back to him: the sweet taste of her tongue, her breathy moans, the feel of her soft lips on his. He broke their kiss and tipped his forehead to hers.

"You're the only one I've ever wanted. No other woman has come close. I've been such an asshole—for not realizing it until I thought it was too late, for not fighting for you even then. I'm sorry for everything I've ever done to make you sad." He'd never had the chance to tell her what had weighed so heavily on him for so many years. Now it was like a huge boulder had lifted from his shoulders and he could finally see what was in front of him and grab it.

She touched her index finger to his lips. "From here on out we're going to live in the present and talk about the future, not go backward. I know why you did it, and I forgive you. Now would you rip my clothes off and make sweet love to me?"

It was all he needed to hear. He shed her shirt and pants from her body as carefully and quickly as he could leaving her bra and panties in place. She hitched up onto her elbows and slid the straps of her bra from her shoulders and released the hook in the back. His gaze locked with hers, and he trailed his hand up her abdomen and slipped it under the loose cup of her bra. As he grazed his thumb over her nipple, she moaned softly, spurring his arousal. His cock was hard and wanting against the zipper of his jeans. He couldn't wait to slip deep inside her pussy, feel her hot, tight walls closing in around him, hear her moaning his name as he thrusted. He only hoped he could last long enough to make it perfect for her, hoped he wouldn't snap and start pounding away like some kind of sex-starved heathen.

Cathy drew her bra off her arms and tossed it to the floor as he pinched a nipple between his thumb and forefinger and his tongue trailed a wet circle around the other.

"Trey. Oh God, Trey. Please." She plucked at his t-shirt, urging him to bare his skin to her.

He rose up and quickly shucked the cotton barrier between them and resumed his attention to her body. She was overwhelmingly beautiful and finally, finally all his.

Cathy threw her head back and resumed her soft pleas for more as he licked and sucked and worshipped her full breasts.

****

Cathy felt like a rocket seconds from takeoff as Trey's hands and mouth worked magic on her breasts. The last time they were together he was clumsy and awkward. The boy was gone, and in his place was a man who knew how to please a woman. She wished she could convince him he didn't need to treat her like a Faberge egg ready to break in his hands. Not that she didn't like to be treated like she meant something, like she *was* something. Spider treated her more like a sex toy than anything else.

She smiled as Trey's mouth ventured lower over her belly, and he looped his thumbs under the band of her panties, whisking the lace from her body. With his palms on her inner thighs he pulled her legs further apart. He stopped and shot her a crooked smile. "You naughty girl," he said and swiped his tongue over her newest piece of jewelry. She had taken Lucy's advice and surprised Spider by getting her clitoral hood pierced. He had barely noticed, but holy stars in heaven, it had enhanced her pleasure by a million. Spider wasn't a fan of going down on her, so this was the first time she'd experienced oral with the jeweled enhancement.

Trey grabbed her ass with both hands and slid her to the edge of the bed, giving him complete access to her slick folds as he dropped to his knees on the floor. He blew softly like he did when he'd mended her fingers. A shiver ran over her body before he settled his hot mouth over her cunt and sucked. His tongue danced over her clit and played with her piercing.

"Oh Trey. Please." She didn't know what the hell she was pleading for, but she ran her hands through his hair and pulled him closer, begging for more. His stubbled cheeks abraded the inside of her thighs as he clamped his hot mouth over her clit, his tongue circling faster and faster until her legs shook. "Oh fuck! Yes, yes, like that. Oh my God!" More swear words and throaty pleas left her mouth like a mantra bringing her closer to the edge.

He began a maddening pattern of delicate licks and nibbles of her clit, followed by the searing heat of his lips sealing around her pussy as he sucked.

"Your mouth is heaven," she said on a long sigh that ended in cry of pleasure as his tongue flicked at her piercing. Her fists tightened around the sheets, toes curled, and she threw her head back. She wanted to hang there on the edge forever, but as much as she wanted to ride the wild, wicked wave of sensation, she could not stop herself from falling.

Bliss rose up, surrounding and consuming every part of her as her climax hit. She screamed his name, but he didn't let up. Instead he broke the suction and licked at the waves of her orgasm until she lay deliriously spent. She was not a religious person, but that was the closest she'd ever come to experiencing a higher energy. He stood while she lay where he left her, panting, her heart raced so fast she felt lightheaded for a second. In the far reaches of her consciousness she heard his cocksure chuckles. Oh, yeah, he had every right to be fucking proud of himself, but now it was her turn to rock his world.

Cathy inched back up to the pillows saying, "One of us has too much clothes on." She licked her lips and nodded to Trey's bottom half.

He unbuttoned his jeans, and they dropped to the floor along with his boxer shorts and, God, was he beautiful. With the exception of a distant streetlight shining through the window, the night they'd slept together as teenagers had been in complete darkness. She had felt the broadness of his shoulders over her body and his length as he moved inside her but she never actually saw him naked. She couldn't help staring as she took him in: broad, tattooed shoulders and chest, ripped six-pack abs, and a dark trail leading to a thick cock waiting to be tasted, to be ridden. She shivered in anticipation.

"It's my turn," she said reaching out and grabbing his hand, coaxing him to the bed. She straddled his lap and flattened her hands on his chest as she kissed him. A primitive instinct made her ache to be stretched and filled as she knew he would, but she held back, instead gliding her slick pussy lips up and down his shaft. The sexy noises he made into her mouth coaxed her on. She snaked her hand to the back of his neck and grabbed a patch of hair near his nape, lifting his chin upward. Working her way down, her tongue ran over his stubbled, salty neck.

A deep moan rumbled from his throat as her hand ventured lower and wrapped around his gorgeous cock. A bead of pre-cum oozed over her fingers. She smeared it over the head and down the sides to the music of his groans.

More. She needed to see and feel more of him. Sitting on her knees, she slid down into the space between his legs and continued to shuttle her hand slowly up and down his length while they locked gazes. Cathy leaned down, lifting her ass in the air. A moment of insecurity reared its ugly head as she recalled all the times Spider told her she had a fat ass. She watched Trey's eyes, which were indeed on her ass, but they weren't filled with judgment.

Fire burned in his eyes as they flicked back to her. "You're so fucking beautiful," he said and ran his fingers through her curls, gathering them away from her face so he could watch her lips take his full length.

Her tongue danced over the head before trailing down his sensitive flesh as she cupped his balls in her hand. She knew she hit his pleasure zone when he tightened his grip on her hair, which threw her own arousal into overdrive. Her eyes tipped to his.

"Fuck," he growled. She arched her brows and swirled the tip of her tongue over the swollen head of his cock, loving the sweet and salty taste of Trey. He hooked his hands under her arms and pulled her up. "If you keep doing that I'll be done in two seconds. As much as I love to be inside your mouth, there's someplace I want to be more." With one hand around her waist, he leaned over and dragged open the nightstand drawer, frantically pawed through the contents, and pulled out a foil square.

"Allow me do the honors." Sliding off him she pinched the packet between her finger and thumb, ripped it open, and took her time to playfully sheathe his fully and beautifully erect cock. Hot and hard and all hers. God, she couldn't wait to sink down on every blessed inch until she could grind herself against the root of him.

"You minx. You're going to pay for that." His lips curled upward, and he flipped her onto her back, nudging her legs apart with his knees.

Or, she thought, a down and dirty missionary fuck might be nice, too, for round one. She was up for any position, any speed, so long as his thick cock was buried inside her soon.

Leaning on one hand planted near her face, Trey fisted himself and teased his head at her opening. The slick sounds betrayed how wet and ready she was for him. Cathy planted a foot on the bed and pushed up to demand more of the delicious stroking.

"What do you want, Cath?" he asked and ran his

finger over her wanting sex, lingering lightly over her clit.

"You. Inside me. Now," she said breathlessly. A moan escaped her throat as he entered her slowly, too slowly. The man was maddening! He caged her face with his arms and captured her stare as her body stretched to accept his impressive breadth and length. He filled her so snugly she lost all sense of where her body ended and his began. She'd be sore in the morning, but damn there was no better souvenir from being with the man she loved.

"You feel so fucking good." His lips brushed hers as she wrapped her legs around his waist, keeping him hostage inside her. Just then she knew she was home in every sense of the word. Their breaths mingled as they found their rhythm, speaking not with words but with their bodies. "I love you, Cathy. I never stopped loving you."

She trailed her fingertips down his back, loving the way it made him shiver. "I love you."

He thrust harder.

"You're my first…" She moaned deep as he hooked his arm around her leg sinking deeper. "…and my only love." And it was the truth. Though she had shared her body with others, Trey had been the only one to have her heart. They moved together, arms and legs tangled and sweaty, gazes locked. "Oh, Trey, yes."

She closed her eyes, and a beautiful burst of stars exploded as she shuddered around his cock. He pumped harder, following her climax, a husky moan filling her mouth until they were both spent. They didn't move for a few moments, his semi-arousal still inside her. He pressed his forehead to hers, and she opened her eyes. His expression took her breath away. So much love and light shone through his eyes.

She caressed his cheek. "Baby, I'm finally home."

Epilogue

Thorn checked the side mirror of the rental moving van she drove. Diesel was keeping a safe following distance in his Dodge Charger, but barely. Behind his beloved vintage car, he towed his equally cherished motorcycle. She didn't need to see inside the car to guess that Dammit had by now worn Diesel down and swapped her backseat for the cushier shotgun spot. Diesel had sworn he wouldn't allow her if she tried, but Thorn knew better. MC ladies might listen politely when told their "place", but that didn't always mean they chose to comply.

The signs flashed by, and after nearly six hours of driving they were approaching Milwaukee, Wisconsin. She was to take the second exit once they passed the city center and head north for another two miles. After that, the plan was to rendezvous in the neighborhood-facing side of the shopping mall's parking lot. There, the Heathens of Milwaukee's first two recruits would be waiting to welcome them and help them move into their temporary digs. Diesel had found the rental on his last recruiting trip. They'd eventually move, knowing his need for privacy, but for now she understood his need to be open and available while building a base.

Nervous excitement bubbled through her veins. After all that had happened in Detroit, all those years of being passed from family to family, of finding, at least temporarily, a home with the Gargoyles, Milwaukee was going to be her new home. With Diesel. As in the old days of their childhood, they were stronger together than apart. Starting the new Heathens' chapter in Milwaukee was their ticket out.

Spider had let her go—he hadn't been in much of a position to argue from his hospital bed. He was out of the woods, but he had a long road to recovery. However, the bitter reality was neither the Gargoyles nor the Heathens of Detroit would ever trust her. That part hurt. She missed Lucy terribly, but her home was with Diesel. The wild boy of her youth who'd taught her to fight the demons of rejection, who'd taught her to love, had never stopped being her true family, even despite the pain he caused her with his terrible sacrifice.

While Spider was still in the hospital, the cops had swept in and arrested several members of the Gargoyles, which effectively put them out of business. They hadn't arrested Spider yet, but Cathy knew it was only a matter of time once his injuries healed. Nevertheless, Diesel had resigned the presidency of the Detroit Heathens. He knew he would have a never-ending and distracting battle dealing with the prejudice against his choice of a former Gargoyle as his old lady. After a unanimous vote, Flint took his place. Flint's very first order as the new leader was to charge Diesel with starting the new Heathens' chapter, a job Diesel accepted with excitement and relief.

Thorn approached her exit and put on her blinker. Diesel did the same. A fresh start lay ahead for them— Thorn and Diesel and Dammit, her family.

The End

www.sandrabunino.com

www.lilashaw.com

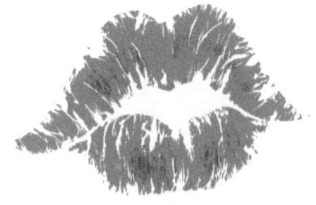

EVERNIGHT PUBLISHING ®

www.evernightpublishing.com